DEDICATION

This book is dedicated to the men in my family who want something different and not want to settle for just anything.

It is also for the women in my family, who want to be ready when they choose the man that comes into their lives and proposes the big question,

"WILL YOU MARRY ME?"

Ephesians 5:23

"For the husband is the head of the wife as Christ is the head of the church, his body, of which he is the Savior." (KJV)

A husband is someone who opens doors and makes a way for his wife. Whatever he gives to a woman, she incubates it and then it multiplies. We must be very careful what we allow a man to give us. If it is good or bad, it will multiply.

The same as the Lord does for us. He opens many doors. It is up to us to enter in and receive from the Lord what He wants us to incubate and then multiply. He has already deposited greatness inside of us for it to increase and spread abroad. The Lord is our Husbandman.

Ladies, we can also build our man up or we can tear him down, so we should be sure that we are in a certain place spiritually, mentally, and physically before we even consider dating, in order to build up the man we choose to be with. *We only date to get to know one another not consummate the relationship.*

When A Man Luvs A Woman

A Novel by

Minister Kathy McClure

Chicago, Illinois

Copyright © 2009

Kathy McClure for McClure Publishing, Inc.

Unless otherwise indicated, all scriptural quotations are from the King James Version (KJV) of the Bible. All references to satan are purposely lower cased, because we give no credit to satan.

The author and publisher have made every effort to ensure the accuracy and completeness of information contained in this book. We assume no responsibility for errors, inaccuracies, omissions, or any inconsistency therein.

Any slights of people, places, belief systems or organizations are unintentional. Any resemblance to anyone living, dead or somewhere in between is truly coincidental.

ISBN-13: 978-0-9790450-7-3

ISBN-10: 0-9790450-7-X

LCCN: 2009908862

Book design by McClure Publishing, Inc.

Editor Rosie Cook

To order additional copies, please contact:
McClure Publishing, Inc.
www.mcclurepublishing.com
800.659.4908
mcclurepublishing@msn.com

Introduction

Women, God will give us to someone who understands that we are godly women. When God walks us down the aisle and gives us to a man that we chose to be with, He gives us to a prepared man. This godly man will know that he does not have to compete with God in our lives. This man will know that if he lines up with God, then we will come to a place to call him, lord, just like Sarah called Abraham, lord.

He will come in the door ready to handle our things as well as his. We will still hold our things together, but he will be able to, just in case we need him. He will be known in the gates of the city. The whole community will celebrate him because of his great wealth. He will have a personal relationship with God that we will understand and allow him to spend time in the presence of the Lord. We will not look at him on the outside but will see into his heart clearly. He will be a man of great stature.

Before a man and a woman get together, there has to be some preparatory skills, giftings, and talents that must be developed before he proposes and she says, "YES!!!" Let's deal with the meaning of the word 'pre.' Pre, according to Merriam-Webster's Dictionary of Law, means "earlier than: prior to: before … preparatory or prerequisite … in advance: beforehand…." It is so important that there is a period before the wedding day where both will know what they like and what they do not like. I believe relationships dissolve because one or the other or both doesn't really know what they want and what they don't want or who they are before crossing the threshold.

I experienced a marriage where we knew we wanted each other, but there were some things about both of us that evolved during the course of the marriage that we noticed we didn't like. Instead of coming to an agreement, we went our separate ways.

This book is not written because I am an expert on marriage; however, it has been written to enlighten those who contemplate getting married and for those who are married and want to remain until DEATH, DO US PART.

We get married under the pretense for better or for worse; for richer or poorer; in sickness and in health; and until death do us part. When the worst, poor, and sickness come, most run into the arms of someone else and give up on the marriage.

Well, God wants us to run into His loving arms. He is the only one that can give us what is best for us. He shows us the treasures in earthen vessels that He placed inside of us. Please don't take me the wrong way. If you are in an abusive relationship - physically, mentally, or emotionally, seek God concerning what you should do and get in a quiet place so that you can hear what He is saying.

When I was going through my divorce, I made the terrible mistake with introducing myself to others as the woman with a broken heart. I wore a big sign in front of me that warned others that I was only invading their space to talk about me and my pain and how I was hurting. At the time, I did not remember that I am spirit first and, therefore, I should have been identifying myself as God's leading lady. Before experiencing divorce, I knew that I was the prize. When it happened, I forgot everything God had placed inside of me in the beginning.

I had a nervous breakdown and couldn't function normally. My thoughts were always on the situation, and I started drinking *like a fish*. Until one day I wrote down my problems in a journal, and then wrote what I heard the Spirit of the Lord saying. I started saying out loud, "I will live and not die and proclaim the Word of the Lord." I am equipped to do mighty exploits, in the earth.

Tommy was lying in bed and his eyes opened before the alarm went off. He was staring at the ceiling thinking about what all he had to do today when suddenly the alarm started buzzing. (BIZZ, BIZZ, BIZZ). He turned off the alarm and turned to look at his wife, Sarah, lying next to him. Thoughts ran through his mind of all the things he had put her through. He started wondering what he could do to make up for the years that he didn't realize who she was.

Sarah was a jack of all trades, and she was a master of many. Everything Sarah said she would do, she did it, and accomplished great things. Tommy admired the way Sarah stuck to getting things done no matter what stood in her way. He felt that she was the most beautiful woman on God's green earth.

After turning to look at Sarah, Tommy touched her on the shoulder and said, "Baby, what can I do for you today? What would make you happy?" He sat up and then leaned over, grabbed her chin and kissed her on her forehead. Then he realized that it was Friday and they both had to go into work.

Reading Tommy's mind as usual, Sarah said, "Let's go to work today and tomorrow morning you can take me to that bed and breakfast restaurant so that we can discuss our new house." For a while now, Sarah had wanted to sell their house and have one built from the ground up – her dream house. She was hoping that Tommy would go along with the idea, but she didn't want to pressure him.

Tommy and Sarah both had well-paying jobs with prestigious companies; Tommy was an electrician and Sarah was a financial consultant. They had made smart investments in the past and fortunately, were in excellent shape financially. But they both knew that you could have all the money in the world and still be unhappy. So,

Tommy and Sarah balanced their lives so that money was not their main focus. They were driven by their love, respect and passion for one another.

TEN YEARS EARLIER

Life was tough for both Sarah and Tommy. They came from similar backgrounds and had experienced similar hardships. Both their parents had been dependent on the State for their income. Their fathers had something in common, too. Unfortunately, they were both alcoholics. Sarah and Tommy lived in the same neighborhood, but never knew each other. Until one day, while entering the grocery store, they literally bumped into each other while going through the door at the same time.

"You need to watch where you're going," Sarah said sassily.

"I'm sorry," Tommy said. "My mother sent me to the store to get some things for dinner. I guess I'm so hungry that it affected my vision and I didn't see you." Tommy grinned.

"My mother sent me to do the same thing," Sarah said. Tommy and Sarah smiled at each other for a long moment until Sarah said, "see you" and walked away.

They went on with their shopping and didn't see each other again until they were leaving the store. "See you," Tommy said. Sarah smiled and they walked off in opposite directions. They both had so many things in common, but really didn't know it at the time. What they both were experiencing was so awful that they didn't want anyone to know. Tommy's father, Ralph, was so angry about how his life was going, that he would beat Tommy's mother, Cindy, until the neighbors would complain and call the Police.

Sarah's father, Jeffrey, was always depending on Sarah's mother, Karen, to get him out of his gambling debts by any means possible. Karen had to do things that she was embarrassed to tell her daughter about. Sarah's mom protected her from this kind of lifestyle, so she would create a life around Sarah that seemed as if everything was fine. Eventually, when Sarah got older, she started hearing rumors from people in the neighborhood about her parents. To make matters worse, the men that her father owed tried to talk to Sarah when she got older. Sarah would cry to her mother, and Karen would still create a life for Sarah that everything was fine. Although, there were times Karen talked to Sarah about reality and told her the truth about how life could really deal you a bad hand.

Cindy, on the other hand, would always tell Tommy about how a man should pray for his wife. Tommy's mother did not wait until he was a man, but she started when he was young because she understood the power of prayer. Tommy promised himself that he would never abuse women. He wanted to know how to love them.

On holidays the family would get together; the women would be in the kitchen cooking, while the men in Tommy's family sat in the living room drinking and watching TV while talking crudely about women. Tommy's father said women were only good for two things – cooking good food and making good loving. "Barefoot and pregnant, that's how I like my woman," one of his uncles joked, as the other men laughed. He made this same comment every time they got together, and every time the other men laughed like it was the first time they'd heard it. Young, impressionable Tommy would sit in the living room listening. Another uncle leaned over to Tommy and told him to put a notch in his belt every time he slept with a different woman.

Tommy's uncles, male cousins, and father would go on and on about all the women they'd had over the years. The more they drank, the more they talked. These men were the only role models that Tommy had. So, when he got older, he decided to follow in their footsteps. Growing up, Tommy thought women were just sex objects. He thought the only reason why God created them was so that men could use them in every way possible, especially in bed. He didn't understand his position and all that it entailed, nor did he want to settle down. Life was good to Tommy because he could have any woman he wanted.

Tommy was on the basketball team in high school; he was the number one most valuable player. He lived to play ball. Every cheerleader wanted to date him, so he decided to date the captain of the cheerleading squad. They were the most popular kids in school and were king and queen of their senior prom.

Things started going downhill for Tommy after high school, so he decided to go to Kaplan College in Cincinnati to complete courses in business and electrical engineering. Tommy didn't have the money he needed to attend college, so he received student loans to help pay for his tuition, books, and room and board. He was discouraged a lot and was tempted to drop out many times.

While attending college, Tommy met lots of women. Now, his life really got worse. He attended all of the parties on and around campus. He was more popular in college than he'd been in high school. Most people liked Tommy because he was very outgoing and seemed to excel at whatever he set his mind to. Tommy knew he wanted to someday settle down and get married, but that was way in the future. In fact, Tommy was trying to get as many notches in his belt as possible so that when he went back home, he could brag to his father and his other male relatives about all of his conquests.

The men in Tommy's family never talked about doing anything meaningful with their lives. They never discussed ways they could improve themselves and the lives of their wives and children. Their main topics of discussion were women and sex. Tommy was under the impression that this was normal conversation for men. He didn't realize that sitting around talking about women and sex only showed how inadequate these men were, how lacking they were in moral character. They equated sexual conquests with manhood, not realizing that one thing had absolutely nothing to do with the other. At the time, Tommy didn't realize that the women in the family were the backbones of these men. The women made up for the qualities that the men were lacking.

Often, men don't realize the impact of what they say has on the little boys who look up to them; how they cling to their every word.

On the other hand, Sarah had grown to be a respectable young woman. She decided to use her grant and scholarship funds to attend St. Mary's College in California. This school specialized in Economics and Business Administration. Sarah received an MBA and Master's degree in Finance. Her specialty was financial analyses and statistics.

Sarah remembered how hard it was for her mother and father to survive on public assistance. She knew that she wanted something better out of life. This drove her to work hard in school and not give up when times became difficult. And times became extremely difficult for Sarah. There were occasions when she only had peanut butter and crackers to eat for breakfast, lunch, and dinner. It was a struggle many days just to keep her laundry clean. The state of California covered her lodging because of her family's lack of income. Being poor had its advantages if you wanted to humble yourself and receive what the government had to offer temporarily. It might not always be the best way; however, you can make the best of it.

While in school, Sarah dated several guys, but those relationships never amounted to anything. They all made promises they couldn't or wouldn't keep. Most of them were looking for one thing and one thing only. Sarah continued playing hard to get in the *sack*. Some guys thought it was a game, so they tried to do everything they could to get her into bed. It never worked though because Sarah saw right through them. There was one time when she almost gave in to temptation, but the phone rang and it was her mother calling to check on her.

Sarah picked up the phone, "Hello."

"It's your mom, honey. How are you doing?"

"Hey mom. It's good to hear from you. Hold on a minute." Sarah put the guy out of her room and told him to call her later. She got back on the phone. "Mom it's really nice to hear your voice."

"Is everything alright?" Karen asked.

"Yes," Sarah said. "I just needed something or someone to intervene; you called at the right time."

"Well, I'm glad I did," Karen replied. "I was just calling to let you know that your father and I will be there for your graduation."

"I can't wait," Sarah said. I've already started packing my things and made arrangements for us to go out."

"I'll call you once we get there," Karen said. "I miss you. I really didn't want you to know that I cried the moment you left, but I knew you were old enough to understand that an education is worth getting."

"Mom," Sarah said, "I really miss you, too. When I was home, I could count on you to be there for me. While I've been here, I had to learn how to depend on myself. Sometimes it got really hard. But the struggles I went through made me stronger. I'll see you tomorrow, mom."

"Bye, sweetie," Karen said.

After talking with her mother, Sarah got ready for bed, excited about the fact that she was graduating the following morning. She had already picked out the clothes she was going to wear and had gotten her hair, pedicure and manicure done earlier that day.

The next morning, after her parents arrived, they all went over to the graduation ceremony. Sarah graduated at the top of her class. She received honors and outstanding merits because of her academic ability.

Her parents took Sarah out to lunch at an upscale restaurant because they were really proud of her. After lunch, they made arrangements to have Sarah's belongings shipped back to the house in Ohio. Sarah's father, Jeffrey, was overprotective of his little girl. He told her that he had gotten her a plane ticket to come back with him and her mother.

On their way back, Jeffrey talked to Sarah about her future and how he expected it to go. He told her that she was not going to waste her life sitting around. He insisted that she was going to look for a job right away.

While Sarah was in school, college scouts came out, but Sarah wasn't interested. Because of her good grades, she could work anywhere, so she setup interviews with several big accounting firms.

The plane landed and they took a taxi home. When they walked in the front door, Sarah realized that there was truly no place like home. She had to get ready that night for her first interview the following day. Sarah knew hitting the pavement wasn't easy because you had to sell yourself in the interview and the employers were looking for specific areas of knowledge in finance. Sarah had no work experience, but was really good at what she knew. She was in the top 10 of her class with a 3.8 Grade Point Average (GPA).

Tommy had to do something in order to graduate on time because he'd spent his sophomore year partying. His poor grades were a mirror reflecting his terrible future if he didn't change his behavior. Tommy woke up in the 3rd semester during his sophomore year and decided to get serious about his education and totally focus, so that he could have a prosperous future. A lot of his friends were smart and knew what it was going to take to get to where they needed to go. They tried many times to convince him to get on track.

There were times when Tommy needed a tutor and some of his friends would step in and help. He wasn't too proud to ask for help. He knew what he had to do.

Tommy made it to graduation by adding more classes each year to his curriculum. Everyone in his family was proud of him. Those that couldn't make the graduation ceremony or the graduation party, sent checks and cash in envelopes that totaled $35,000. Tommy used some of the money to pay back part of his student loans, and the other part to get him an apartment. He didn't want to return home to live with his parents. Tommy had gotten used to living by himself.

When Sarah got back home, she realized how much things had changed. Her father didn't drink any more and he had stopped gambling. Sarah was delighted about the changes in her father. Her parents seemed to be getting along great. They both wanted Sarah to see that they were really good parents, but had experienced some difficult times. They wanted to prove to Sarah that a good marriage could survive all difficulties.

That night after they'd settled in, they talked about the good times Sarah had while she was away at school. Karen told Sarah she would get up to fix breakfast every morning so that Sarah would have the energy needed for interviewing.

The following morning, Sarah ran downstairs and found her mother standing at the stove cooking, while her father was sitting at the table reading a newspaper and drinking coffee. She said "good morning," then walked over, kissed her dad on the jaw, then kissed her mother on her neck. "I'm really ready to get hired today at the first firm I interview with," she said. "My attitude is to win."

"That's right baby," Jeffrey said. You have the right attitude. Just *take the bull by the horns* and run with it. Your mother and I are proud of you for finishing school and graduating at the top of your class."

"You've outshone many," Karen added. "I can only imagine what you're going to do when you start working. I've never had to work. Your dad always took care of me."

Sarah said, "I want both of you to know that no matter what we went through, everything is going to be uphill from here."

Karen placed Jeffrey and Sarah's plates on the table.

"Mom, this breakfast looks delicious. But don't be mad if I don't eat all of it. I'm real excited about my job interview."

Karen said, "Not to worry. I just want to make sure you won't have hunger pains or a growling stomach during your interview. I also called a cab to take you to your interview. It should be here in about 20 minutes."

Sarah laughed. "Mom, you are the greatest."

Jeffrey started eating right away because he had to leave for work soon.

After Sarah took a couple of bites, she ran upstairs to get her purse and suit jacket. The cab pulled up in front of the house and honked.

"Bye mom; bye dad," Sarah said. I'll let you know what happens."

The cab got Sarah there in no time. He pulled up in front of a skyscraper made of glass. It was beautiful. The warm colors drew Sarah into the revolving door and stopped at the Security Desk to check in. After receiving security clearance, she looked around to see what elevator bank she should take.

As soon as Sarah walked into the offices of Lancing Caruthers & Associates Inc., CPA's, the receptionist said, "We were expecting you." She buzzed the interviewer, Mr. Weathers, to let him know Sarah had arrived. Mr. Weathers came out to meet her and loved her demeanor. He already was impressed that she graduated with a 3.8 GPA. Before the interview was finished the interviewer asked Sarah, "when can you start?"

Almost losing her composure, Sarah said, "next Monday," because she didn't want to come across as being too anxious. Although inside her stomach her spirit was leaping for JOY.

When Sarah left the building, she immediately called her mother on her cell phone. "Mom," she said excitedly, "I got the job."

"That's wonderful," Karen said, sounding just as excited as Sarah. "So, when do you start?"

"Next Monday," Sarah answered. I'm going to get together with some friends this weekend to celebrate. Do you want to come?"

"Thanks for the invite," Karen said. "But you guys go ahead and have fun. We'll have our own special celebration. I want to have some mother-daughter time together."

"Okay mom. I'm on my way home. All this excitement is exhausting," Sarah said, laughing.

This was definitely a reason to celebrate. Sarah called some of her old friends to go out to a nearby club to help celebrate landing a position at one of the biggest, oldest and most prestigious accounting firms in Ohio, Lancing Caruthers & Associates Inc., CPA's.

Sarah invited Jessica, Sheila, Rita and Carol, four of her oldest and dearest friends to celebrate with her. They were meeting Robert, Jeff and Troy at the club. DJ Quick was playing that night, and he was in the mood to play like he never played before.

That same night Tommy decided to go out with a couple of friends. As he was walking in the door of the club, Sarah was walking in at the same time. They bumped into each other and Sarah said, "You need to watch where you're going."

"That voice sounds familiar," Tommy said. They looked at each other and remembered this same incident happened when they were younger. They both laughed.

"It must be meant for us to know each other because we keep bumping into one another," Sarah exclaimed.

"Either that or you need glasses," Tommy said teasingly. "I can't believe you didn't see this fine hunk of a man walking next to you."

"What fine hunk of a man?" Sarah asked, glancing around quickly. "Where he is?" She turned back to Tommy, grinning. "And you're the one who needs glasses, if you didn't notice the finest woman that God placed on this green earth walking in next to you."

They stared at each other with serious expressions for a few moments, and then burst into laughter.

Tommy asked, "Can I ask you to dance later?"

"Sure," Sarah said "You can help me celebrate."

"What are you celebrating?"

Sarah said, "I'll tell you later. It was good *bumping* into you again."

"I'll see you later then," Tommy said, taking a twenty-dollar bill from his pocket and handing it to Sarah. "Have a couple of drinks on me."

"Thank you," Sarah said with an appreciative smile before walking away to find her friends.

This was a nice club because the atmosphere was classy, yet down to earth at the same time. The customers were diverse and from various backgrounds and everybody had the same goal – to have a good time.

The club also had a restaurant attached where people were able to order food. There was also a beauty salon on the other side, so a guy could get his hair cut and a woman could get her hair styled. Some people wanted to look good at the club with a fresh hairdo. Business was great. No matter what was going on in the economy, this club was doing better than most.

Sarah was working on her third shot of tequila when she started looking around for Tommy. She felt like hitting the dance floor. After scanning the room for a second time, she turned her head and there was Tommy, his face very close to hers.

"Looking for me?" he said, a grin spread across his handsome face.

Sarah flinched with surprise, then smiled.

Would you like to dance?" Tommy asked.

"I thought you'd never ask," Sarah said, still smiling. She loved a man who could make her smile. "How did you know?"

"I've been watching you for most of the evening. I was waiting for the right moment." He paused. "This feels like the right moment to me." He paused again, his smile widening, examining her face. "Does it feel like the right moment to you, Sarah?"

"Definitely," Sarah said, her smile widening to equal Tommy's as she reached out her hand to him. Tommy grabbed Sarah's hand and led her to the dance floor.

DJ Quick was playing Reggae that night. Sarah loved to dance to Reggae music. Tommy was amazed at how Sarah could move her body. Her eyes were closed and she danced like she was in her own little world. Tommy was a pretty good dancer himself. He was able to talk Sarah into dancing with him again that night, although, it didn't take too much convincing. Sarah loved to dance and she especially loved dancing with Tommy. There were lots of other things she liked about Tommy, too.

After that night, Tommy and Sarah started dating. They both felt that there was a reason why they kept bumping into one another. It was God causing destiny to take place.

Weeks later, Tommy helped Sarah move into her condo on the 33rd floor in a high rise on 1122 9th Street in Cleveland, Ohio. They first went over to get the place in order before the furniture was delivered. They didn't have much to do. Sarah just wanted to clean the rooms and prepare the place for how she wanted it to look and smell. Sarah plugged a Glade® Clean Linen plug-in in every room of the condo. She loved the way it smelled. Over the fireplace, she placed candles of the same scent.

Tommy was going to stay during the day to wait for the furniture because Sarah had to work. Tommy thought that Sarah had good taste in clothes, furniture and in her choice of automobile. She was driving a 2009 Audi TT-RS. He knew this was a very classy woman he was dealing with.

Sarah gave Tommy the keys and told the doorman that Tommy would be there in the morning waiting for the furniture to arrive. Later that evening, Tommy had already made plans to take Sarah to dinner.

When the furniture arrived Tommy wasn't sure where to have them set it up, but he came up with a nice layout. They could always change it later, he thought. After he was done, he left and went to his place to prepare for the evening.

Sarah got home from work and really liked how Tommy had arranged the furniture. She settled in and relaxed before Tommy came to pick her up for dinner. At first, Sarah was looking forward to going out with him.

When Tommy arrived to pick Sarah up for their date, she opened the door with a strange look on her face. She wasn't feeling well and really wanted to cancel, probably because she was nervous. But Tommy talked her into going in spite of how she was feeling. For some reason, Sarah was having second thoughts about dating Tommy. Perhaps it was because she'd heard rumors at the club about his reputation as a lady's man. But she really liked Tommy, so she decided not to dwell on those rumors, and asked if he could wait for her to get dressed.

Sarah had already taken a shower and had applied her makeup; she had styled her hair as if she were going to a ball. Her goal was to make sure that Tommy was totally mesmerized by her beauty.

Tommy sat down in a chair in the living room. Sarah had the peaceful sounds of Kenny G playing softly. She walked toward her bedroom, thinking *I hope he doesn't try to come into my room while I'm getting dressed.* Although Sarah trusted Tommy, she still had her guard up. She closed her bedroom door and locked it just to be on the safe side.

Sometimes, one bad relationship makes you look at other relationships the same way. You try to get over it, but somehow something a person says or does triggers memories from the past, and the ghosts from the past relationships begin to haunt you.

About 20 minutes later, Sarah walked out of her bedroom and Tommy's mouth dropped open. He froze for at least two minutes and hoped she didn't notice. Sarah smiled and thought to herself, *my plan is working already. He's mesmerized.*

"Are you okay, Tommy," Sarah asked, pleased and a little amused at the affect she was having on him.

Tommy blinked his eyes several times to get himself together. He couldn't believe he'd reacted that way. He had always been the *cool* one. "Sure. I'm fine. Let's go," he said, rising from the sofa, trying to sound as if he was unaffected by Sarah's beauty.

Tommy wanted this date to be special. He wanted to make sure it was a night that neither of them would soon forget. He took Sarah to Jay's Seafood Restaurant located in the Historical Oregon District off the Southeast edge of Downtown Dayton.

While driving to the restaurant, Sarah thought this would be a good time to try and learn more about Tommy — his likes and dislikes — and what she needed to do to make him like her. The chemistry was already there.

"So, talk to me," Sarah said. "Tell me what's on your mind?"

"Well, actually," Tommy said, "I'm thinking about what I can do to convince you that I'm the right man for you, Sarah. I know you have second thoughts about me, but at the same time, you want to have a relationship with me."

Sarah said, "Tommy, please don't try to read me because you just might be wrong, you know," while saying to herself, *I think I'm in love with this man already, but I don't want to show him because I've been hurt in the past, and I don't want to make the same mistake again.*

Tommy continued, "Sarah, it's time for me to get focused. I've done a lot of things in my past. Some I regret, and others I've learned from. Give me time to show you that I can give you everything you're looking for in a man."

"That's just what I wanted to hear," Sarah said, smiling. "I finished school and I've landed a great position. My next goal is to have someone in my life that I can spend time with. But I have to give this some more thought. Okay?"

"Well, for tonight let's just enjoy each other's company and see where it goes from here. Let's take it a day at a time."

Sarah knew that Tommy was telling her to keep things in perspective; to try not to determine the future of a relationship based on a single date. And she knew he was right. In the past, she'd assumed things about men from the way they'd behaved on the first few dates and by how much she had enjoyed herself with them. But she had learned that most men are on their best behavior during their initial pursuit of a woman. But later, after she had gotten to know them, after the excitement and thrill of the pursuit had passed (during which time they were going out of their way trying to impress her), they revealed their true selves. And, sadly, Sarah had always been disappointed.

Sarah remembered her mother telling her that men think one way while women put so much more into the relationship. Karen would always tell her daughter to trust God. *He will show you signs, and you will know in your spirit if he is feeling you the way you are feeling him.*

When they arrived at Jay's Seafood Restaurant, the valet walked to the driver's side of the car. Tommy rolled down his window and handed the valet his key. Tommy was driving a black Infiniti two-door with a gray tone interior, wood grain, XM radio, GPS system, sunroof, fully loaded. The valet driver opened Tommy's car door and Tommy showed Sarah that he was a true gentleman. He got out of the car, walked quickly to the passenger side, opened the door, and extended his hand to help her out of the car. Smiling, and also somewhat impressed, Sarah took Tommy's hand and stepped out of the car. Tommy shut the door and led her to the restaurant. When they got inside, the maître d' greeted them with a smile.

"A table for two reserved under Whitfield," Tommy said.

"Follow me. I'll put you in the best seat in the restaurant," the maître d' said. Sarah glided across the floor in her Prada shoes. The maître d' pulled out her chair, picked up her napkin, placed it gently and neatly on her lap, and then handed her a menu. Tommy sat down across from Sarah and stared into her eyes. *My goodness, Sarah thought. This man really looks good.* The intimacy between Tommy and Sarah was so palpable that the maître d' felt it. It hovered over their table like it had a life of its own. He smiled to himself as he handed Tommy his menu and walked away.

As they were looking over the menu, Sarah was wondering what ingredients were in the crab cakes. Their waiter came over, introduced himself, and then placed a basket of homemade bread and honey butter in the middle of the table, and a glass of water in front of each of them. He continued with a list of special dishes that the chef prepared for the day, then asked them what they'd like to drink.

"Can you tell me what the ingredients are in the crab cakes?" Sarah asked. She'd been to Baltimore once and the crab cakes she'd eaten there were absolutely the best she'd ever tasted. The waiter said that he'd ask the chef to come and talk to her. Before he walked away, Tommy asked for a bottle of their best merlot.

"Would you mind if I order for you?" Tommy asked Sarah.

"Sure," Sarah said smiling. She'd never had a man order her meal before. She thought there was something sweet and sophisticated about it.

The chef approached the table and began telling Sarah what was in the crab cakes. After he finished, she smiled and said, "I really like the service in this restaurant. You have time to cook *and* meet the requests of your customers. I'm really impressed."

The chef smiled his appreciation of Sarah's comment. Tommy thanked him and told him that they were ready to order.

"I'll get your waiter," the chef said, graciously. "Enjoy your meal."

"I think I'll have the crab cakes to start with," Sarah said.

"What would you like for your main dish?" Tommy asked.

Sarah studied the menu for a few moments. "I'm not sure yet." She looked up at him. "I'm thinking the appetizers might be enough."

Tommy shook his head. "I brought you here for a full course meal. Hopefully, one of the most delicious you've ever had." He smiled to let Sarah know that he wasn't putting down her idea. He just wanted to please her.

Sarah returned his smile. "Okay. Fine. How about we get one main dish and share it?"

"Now that sounds like a plan," Tommy said.

When Sarah suggested the lobster plate, Tommy appeared somewhat surprised "That's just what I was going to suggest. Are you reading my mind already? I see I'm going to have to keep my eye on you." Grinning and looking into Sarah's big, beautiful, brown eyes, Tommy felt a warm sensation in his stomach.

The waiter returned and asked if they were ready to order.

"We sure are," Tommy said. "*My lady* would like the crab cakes appetizer."

Sarah felt a warm feeling in her chest, close to her heart, when Tommy said the words "my lady." *Slow down, girl,* she warned herself. *Those are just words.*

"And I'd like the hot gumbo," Tommy continued. For our main course, we'd like the Lobster Platter with two plates, please."

The waiter memorized the order. "Can I get you something more to drink, sir?"

"Not right now," Tommy said. "But when the main course comes, I'm sure we'll be ready for another bottle of merlot." The waiter nodded and Tommy thanked him before he walked away.

"Can I ask you a question?" Sarah said.

Tommy smiled. "You can ask me anything."

Sarah didn't respond right away. She wanted to ask her question in a way so that Tommy didn't think she was desperate to be in a relationship with him. "What are you looking for in a relationship?" she asked.

Tommy thought for a moment. "Well, I'm looking for a woman that I can give something to and she will multiply it and assist me with building the business that I have in mind."

*Assist you? S*he thought to herself. Then she thought, *give the man a chance to explain what he means.* "Assist you in building your business?" she asked. "What kind of assistance do you need?"

"I need someone in my corner to help me in areas where I lack." Tommy looked up to heaven and then looked back at her. He continued, "I'd like a woman that I can share things with. I want a woman that I can trust implicitly."

I like that, Sarah thought. Being able to truly trust the man she was with was very important to her, too. "I see," she said, then allowed Tommy to continue.

"So, what are you looking for in a man?" Tommy asked, turning Sarah's question around on her.

Sarah said, "I'm looking for someone I can depend on. And like you, someone that I can totally trust. Someone who won't be tempted by any and every woman that walks by."

Tommy thought about some of his past relationships. He admitted that he hadn't treated the women very nice or respectfully. He dated them for a while, and then when he became bored, or someone he thought was better came along, dropped them like a hot potato. He was hoping that if he fell in love with Sarah, that she wouldn't treat him the way he had treated those women.

Another waiter came out with the appetizers and placed Sarah's dish on the table in front of her. She looked at the crab cakes, and inhaled the mouthwatering aroma. "Mmmmmmm," she said. "They smell so good."

Tommy smiled. He loved it when a woman was happy. It made him happy. In his heart, the way he had treated women in the past truly bothered him.

The waiter returned and placed Tommy's gumbo in front of him. "Thank you," Tommy said. The service in the restaurant was truly excellent; that's why he'd brought Sarah here. Yes, he had wanted to impress her. But he also wanted her to have the best – the best food, the best service, the best atmosphere. Tommy really liked Sarah and he was hoping that in time she'd feel the same way about him (if she didn't already). He was really looking forward to getting to know her better.

When they were finished with their appetizers, Sarah excused herself to go to the ladies room. While looking in the bathroom mirror and checking her make-up, she couldn't stop herself from smiling.

Tommy sat at the table wondering what Sarah thought so far about him. He couldn't imagine what was going on in her head. He had learned a long time ago that you never really knew what a woman was thinking, and that there was no point in even speculating.

When Sarah returned to the table, Tommy stood up and held out her chair. Sarah got that warm feeling in her chest again. He was such a gentleman. She liked that.

As soon as Tommy sat back down, his cell phone rang.

He asked Sarah if she minded if he took the call. "It might be business."

"Sure. Go right ahead," Sarah said, pleased that he'd asked if she minded.

But Tommy knew by the number that flashed on his cell phone screen, that it wasn't a business call.

"Hello," Tommy spoke softly into his phone.

It was Nicole, "Hi Tommy."

"What can I help you with this evening?" Tommy asked.

"I was hoping that we could get together next Saturday for a cookout at my parents' house," Nicole said.

"I have to check my schedule and get back to you," Tommy said.

"Okay. Let me know," she said. "Bye."

Tommy hung up the phone.

The call somewhat bothered Sarah for a portion of the evening. She was almost positive that it hadn't been a "business call."

Tommy could tell something was wrong. And Tommy needed to get Sarah back into her previous mood, laughing and talking. He had to get rid of the tiny cloud that had appeared in their sunny atmosphere. "That was a friend of mine," he told Sarah. "She invited me to a cookout next Saturday, but I wanted to check with you first to see if you were free."

Sarah was happy that he wanted her to meet his friends. *This is a good sign*, she thought. "I don't think I have any plans for next Saturday," she said, trying not to sound too eager. I'd love to go."

The next waiter came out with the main course along with another bottle of merlot. Sarah felt so good that she started feeding Tommy as if he were a baby boy who didn't know how to use utensils.

Tommy thought, *no one has ever fed me*. This kind of made Tommy feel that Sarah really knew how to treat her man.

When the bill came, Tommy paid with a credit card and left a large tip. *Wow*, Sarah thought. *He's generous too.* She remembered going on a date where the guy didn't tip the waiter at all and had complained all night about how expensive the food was.

The night was still young and Tommy thought it might be nice to take a walk and continue their conversation. It was a beautiful night and the temperature was perfect for walking.

As they were strolling away from Jay's Restaurant, Tommy grabbed Sarah's hand and pulled her to him. "Sarah," he said, "I had a good time tonight. I hope that we can do this again soon." He smiled. "Real soon."

"I had a good time, too," Sarah said. "I'd like to see you again." Sarah thought about what had happened with her last relationship where the guy knew her every move. He studied her and knew her routine. We are creatures of habit. Once we create a certain routine, we pretty much follow it. This guy knew when she was coming and when she was going. He took advantage of it and used it against Sarah.

Sarah tried hard not to remember her past relationships, but no matter how she tried, her past experiences kept interfering with the present. She tried very hard not to hold against Tommy what other guys had put her through. Some guys took Sarah's kindness for weakness, and that was their mistake.

Sarah was a kindhearted young woman. But she was also extremely strong. And it angered her when she felt she was being used or taken advantage of. Those men who mistreated Sarah had learned that she was not the weak, timid little thing that they thought she was.

One evening when Sarah was in college, her boyfriend called her to pick her up for a dinner date. She got ready and was excited about going out. She had studied and worked really hard on a book report, so going out to dinner would really help her relax. The guy was an hour late. By the time he got there he had someone else in the car stating that he had to drop her off. Sarah looked inside the car and said no thanks. She was so angry that she went inside and fixed herself some chamomile tea to relax and fall off to sleep. She never dealt with this guy again.

Sarah and Tommy walked back to his car. He opened her door, ran to the other side and jumped in. They cruised to Sarah's place.

Instead of going up, Tommy just walked Sarah to her door. He'd decided that he wanted this relationship to be different from all the others. He didn't want to take advantage of her. For the first time in his life, he wanted to be a good man and not a player.

Tommy felt good about this relationship. He felt that he wanted to take it to the next level. But there were some people in Tommy's life he had to let go before he and Sarah could really become closer. The women he was seeing were just platonic relationships. He thought Sarah might not understand the relationships and put more into them than what was actually going on.

Tommy drove home feeling like a new man.

The following day while Tommy was at work, he felt Sarah all in his spirit. It was as if she had entered his heart. A man needs a woman he can confide in. One he can truly trust. He knew he'd only known Sarah a short while, but he felt that way about her. If a man shares something with you, opens his heart to you, do not share it with anyone but God.

He felt that Sarah was someone he could depend on; someone who would always be there for him.

Sarah was trained to be this way when she was growing up. No matter how difficult it got, Sarah's mom was there for her father.

Tommy experienced what he was taught. He started feeling how vain it was not to have a woman he called his own.

In the beginning, in the garden of Eden, God saw that it is not good for man to be alone, so He made him a helpmate suitable for him. (Genesis 2:18) It was God's original plan for a man to leave his mother and father and cleave to his wife. (Genesis 2:24; Ephesians 5:21) It was God's original plan that a man and a woman would get together to be a family and replenish and multiply the earth.

By midday, Tommy was still feeling Sarah after their dinner at the restaurant. He sat behind his desk hoping that Sarah would sense he was thinking about her and call him. He didn't want to bother her because she'd told him that she was very busy at work. Then suddenly his phone rang. He looked at the caller ID and saw it as Sarah. Tommy didn't answer until the third ring because he didn't want to seem too anxious.

"Hello, this is Tommy speaking."

"Hi Tommy, this is Sarah. I was just calling to see how your day was going. I wanted to talk with you before I got too busy."

"Well, I was working on some paperwork. At around 1:30 p.m., I have to go and install some electrical wires, some circuit breakers, and a central air unit in this building before the purchaser stops by. I want to bring it up to code," Tommy said, giving Sarah a run down of how his day will be going.

Sarah stopped what she was doing and gave Tommy her undivided attention. She knew that a man liked a woman who really listened to him, even if the conversation was about something that didn't interest her. How would it be if a KING decreed a law and no one listened? It's the same when it comes to a man. He wants his family to listen to what he has to say. When the family ignores him, he feels as if he is not being respected as the man of the house. And he might be tempted to go and find someone who makes him feel like the *man* that his family doesn't.

A woman on the other hand, wants to be able to depend on her man. She wants to be able to know, that whatever he says he's going to do, he'll do it. When a man doesn't keep his word, it leaves the woman feeling that she can't trust what he says. And a relationship without trust, cannot survive.

In Sarah's past, men would make promises that they wouldn't keep. So, she started feeling like she could only depend on herself and became very independent.

The issues of life come from the heart and we speak it out of our mouths and then it is supposed to manifest around us. Our actions must line up with what we say we are going to do. When we speak it, it must come to pass. This is the power of the tongue (Proverbs 18:21).

"Tommy, my other line is ringing," Sarah said. "I'll call you later to see what our schedule looks like for this evening."

Sarah was already speaking about them as a couple. You see, what she spoke in his ear gate, "our schedule," can become a reality. We should confirm the relationship in our conversations. If couples are still speaking in a singular tense, then that is one of the reasons they will continue to be, single.

"Okay," Tommy said. "Have a good day. If I don't hear from you, I'll call you at home this evening."

"Alright bye, honey," Sarah said.

Tommy said, "Bye."

Sarah rushed home from work to jump in the shower and settle in before calling Tommy. It had started raining and thundering outside. Sarah hoped that Tommy wouldn't decide to stay in because of the weather.

After talking with Sarah earlier, Tommy's day hadn't gone as he'd hoped. The buyer said he would settle the closing the next day because he had another appointment that couldn't be rescheduled. Tommy had been disappointed. He was not only an electrician; he also purchased buildings, rehabbed them up, and sold them to make a profit.

Sarah's phone rang and it was Tommy. He told her that he'd had a bad day and he really needed to talk to her about it. Sarah told him to stop by. Then she prepared a quick, easy meal.

It seemed as if Tommy was right around the corner because he arrived shortly after the phone call. The doorman called to see if Sarah was expecting company and she told him to let Tommy up. Sarah could tell right away that Tommy was feeling a little blue; although to Sarah, the rain made the evening very romantic. Sarah had candles burning, which made the place feel warm and inviting.

Tommy sat on the couch and picked up the remote control. He turned to a football game and asked Sarah if she had a problem with it.

"No," Sarah said. "I love to hear sports playing throughout the house. Although I'm not really interested in sports, I still want my man to be able to watch them."

Tommy was glad to hear this because he was a really big sports fan.

Sarah asked him if he wanted dinner to be served in the living room. Tommy liked that because he wanted to be casual that night. Sarah told Tommy whenever he was ready to talk about his day, she was ready to listen.

Tommy had changed his mind. He didn't feel like talking about it anymore. "I really don't want to discuss it right now," he said. But I'm glad that you're willing to listen." Being with Sarah had made him forget about the lousy day he'd had. He just wanted to enjoy the evening, watch the game, and be with Sarah.

After the game ended, Tommy kissed Sarah on her forehead and left.

The Saturday at Nicole's Family Cookout:

Tommy picked up Sarah and they drove over to Nicole's house for the cookout. You could smell the barbecue cooking a mile away. Nicole and her parents were good cooks. Nicole's father had been a chef in the army. He learned how to cook a lot of southern dishes. The backyard was acres of land and the landscaping was well manicured. They had expensive yard furniture as if they entertained people all the time. Nicole also hired a DJ who played music from different eras. He was inside the studio they designed in their basement. The sound system was wired to play throughout the house and in the backyard. Nicole's father made sure he turned off the timer for the sprinkler so that it wouldn't automatically come on while they were entertaining.

Tommy immediately took Sarah over to introduce her to Nicole's family. Nicole had a few friends already there, so she introduced them to Tommy and Sarah. One of the girls they were introduced to was TerriLynn. When Nicole introduced Tommy and Sarah to TerriLynn, TerriLynn behaved as if Sarah wasn't even there. She told Tommy it was nice to meet him, then winked her eye at him. Sarah pretended not to notice because she didn't want to create a scene. This was her first time with Tommy's friends, so she wanted to make a good impression. Nicole immediately noticed and pulled Tommy and Sarah away to look at some family pictures inside the house.

Sarah told Nicole that she had to use the bathroom and Nicole told her where it was. Sarah thanked her and walked down the hall where Nicole had indicated.

"Sarah seems like a really nice young lady," Nicole said to Tommy. "How did you meet her?"

Tommy smiled. "We kept bumping into each other, *literally*, and one thing led to another." He laughed as he remembered the first time he and Sarah had met.

TerriLynn was keeping her eye on Tommy, waiting for the chance to catch him alone. Later that evening, when Sarah went to the bathroom again, TerriLynn had her chance. She rushed over to where Tommy was sitting. She smiled her sexiest smile, slipped her phone number into his pocket and told him to call her.

Tommy really didn't want to deal with TerriLynn because of how she came on to him while he was with his woman. He felt she was a little too forward. He never wanted to cheat on Sarah. But TerriLynn was extremely attractive, and it was hard to resist the temptation.

The food was ready and everyone was going along the serving table, preparing their plates. Some sat down to eat while others stood around talking and enjoying the delicious food. There was about 65 people there, but TerriLynn didn't see anyone but Tommy. She didn't want to seem obvious to Sarah, so she stayed away for the rest of the evening until it was time to go. She stood with Nicole and her parents waving good-bye as Tommy and Sarah pulled off.

Sarah's job kept her extremely busy. She had three new billion dollar clients and had to keep up with their financial books. Tommy knew this and decided to take advantage of the situation. He eventually called TerriLynn and set up a date with her. Tommy had started feeling that

Sarah was too busy trying to impress her boss to spend time with him.

Everything TerriLynn said was what Tommy needed to hear at the time. She wore clothes that were extremely seductive and left very little to the imagination. Every time Tommy saw TerriLynn his heart would beat rapidly. She excited his soul. TerriLynn knew this, so every time she saw Tommy, she made sure that each outfit was sexier than its predecessor, her hair was always done, and her makeup was meticulous. And she was always very adoring; clinging to his every word when he spoke. Tommy had no idea that she had plans to destroy his relationship with Sarah. She wanted him for herself and she was going to have him.

TerriLynn had never had a man of her own; she always dealt with someone else's man. Because of her past lifestyle, she knew it was time for her to deal with a good man. Now, she was determined to find a good man to take care of her since she had been used in the past.

TerriLynn never talked about herself. She always pumped Tommy up and made him believe that he was the most interesting and exciting man she'd ever met. She knew information about him that Tommy didn't know. It is amazing how you can pretty much find out everything you want to know about a person if you are willing to pay for it. This was not TerriLynn's first time doing this. She learned early on to do a background check on men. She stopped going by what they told her about themselves. Her experience with Marc had taught her a lot.

Marc was a young man who was always down on his luck. Whatever he touched seemed to crumble in his hands. He was a psychopathic liar who told girls whatever he thought they wanted or needed to hear. Nothing seemed to work for him, until he met TerriLynn. Marc knew that women found him attractive and he used that to his advantage. He was 6′3″ and weighed about 210 lbs. He had a smooth dark complexion and wore nice clothes; but no one ever knew what he did for a living. When TerriLynn would ask him about it, he would tell her that he'd inherited some money from one of his family members and then he would quickly change the subject.

TerriLynn loved Marc, so she believed him. And, she stopped questioning him. But he led her down a path of pain and destruction, until she finally ran away from him. TerriLynn was devastated by the way Marc had treated her. She became hardened and distrustful. She promised herself that she would not be hurt or used again. She would take whatever she wanted. She would find a man to take care of her the way she felt she deserved to be taken care of. And she didn't care if that man belonged to somebody else.

TerriLynn was 5′9″ and 125 lbs. She wore high heels, which made her legs look long and sexy. Her caramel colored skin was flawless, and she had light brown, silky hair. After TerriLynn left Marc, she went to school to become a nurse. She was working at Christ hospital in Cincinnati, Ohio. But TerriLynn was tired of working. It was time for her to be taken care of. And, she had chosen Tommy to be her caretaker.

*   *   *

Sheila and Robert were friends of Sarah. They both worked for the same not-for-profit organization that organized charitable fund raising events to promote cancer research. Sarah bought two tickets to their next event for her and Tommy. She hadn't seen Tommy in a while and was looking forward to the evening, especially since it was for a good cause. She bought a new dress and shoes for the occasion and had gotten her hair done that morning; she wanted to look good for Tommy.

The night of the event, Tommy had an emergency project and was at work until 8:30 p.m. The event started at 9:00 p.m., so he called Sarah and told her he was running late. Sarah told him that she would take a cab and he could meet her there; she told him she would leave his ticket at the door.

Sarah found herself seated at a table with three couples. They were very friendly, but she felt a bit uncomfortable being the only single woman at the table. There were two empty chairs at the table; one of them was for Tommy. She wondered who would be sitting in the other chair.

Sarah watched a woman in a tight red dress slowly make her way towards the table. She watched the heads of several men turn in her direction. Sarah recognized the woman immediately; it was TerriLynn, the woman she'd met at Nicole's barbecue. *What's she doing here?* she wondered. The short, extremely tight, low-cut red dress she wore, in Sarah's opinion, revealed way too much of her ample assets. TerriLynn sat down in the empty chair next to the one Sarah was saving for Tommy. She didn't speak to anyone at the table. She set her drink on the table, crossed her legs and looked around like she was searching for somebody.

Tommy arrived about an hour later and Sarah had never been happier to see him. He kissed her on the cheek, apologized for being late, and told her she looked beautiful. Sarah noticed that TerriLynn looked suddenly annoyed. She picked up her glass, downed the rest of her drink, set the glass down hard on the table. She rose quickly and noisily from her chair, and sashayed away from the table. Nobody at the table seemed to mind her departure.

Sarah was having a wonderful time. The food was delicious and the band was excellent. She and Tommy spent a lot of time on the dance floor. One time, when she and Tommy were slow dancing, she glanced over his shoulder and noticed TerriLynn, who was standing a few feet away from the dance floor, glaring at her. She smiled and hugged Tommy even closer, until TerriLynn turned away.

Later that night, Sarah was surprised when she saw Peter Stamply. She hadn't realized that they knew some of the same people. She'd met Peter at a nightclub called The Caplan's a few months ago when she'd gone out with her girlfriends; she'd just started dating Tommy at the time. She had enjoyed talking to Peter, had danced with him a few times, (he was a good dancer) and had to admit that she found him attractive, and knew that the feeling was mutual. Peter recognized her also and when Tommy walked over to talk to some friends, she and Peter chatted for a while. She found out that Peter was a friend of someone who worked with Sheila and Robert. Later, when Tommy asked her who Peter was, she told him he was a man she worked with. She felt a little guilty about not telling Tommy the truth, but thought that if she told him that she'd met Peter at a club, he might have gotten the wrong idea. Plus, she had done nothing wrong. When Peter had asked for her phone number that night she'd told him that she was seeing someone.

TerriLynn behaved like she had at the barbecue. She came back to the table later, smiling, obviously having had too much to drink, and talked to Tommy, but ignored Sarah completely. Sarah wondered why the woman didn't like her, and then came to the conclusion that she was just rude. Some women were like that when it came to other women. But Sarah decided that she wasn't going to let it ruin her night. She was just glad to be spending time with Tommy; they hadn't been out in a while.

Later on she saw TerriLynn and Peter talking to each other. *Good*, she thought, *that'll keep her away from Tommy*. Sarah was neither blind nor naïve. She could tell by the way TerriLynn looked at Tommy that she was attracted to him. And, although she had grown to trust Tommy completely, she didn't trust TerriLynn one bit.

TerriLynn sat at the table alone, fuming, staring at the couples on the dance floor, which included Tommy and Sarah. She knew Tommy had been surprised to see her. She'd called him earlier in the week about getting together that night and he'd told her that he was going to a benefit with a friend.

TerriLynn assumed it was the benefit that she had already purchased a ticket from Nicole without mentioning it to Tommy. Nicole's parents worked on the committee with Robert and Sheila.

She had put on her sexist dress and heels and had spent all afternoon at the spa getting pampered with a facial and a massage, a manicure and a pedicure. She knew she looked especially good that night and that Tommy was going to be happily surprised to see her. But she had felt sick when she saw Sarah sitting at the table. And she'd felt even sicker when Tommy showed up and acted like he didn't even see her while fawning all over Sarah. But when she came back to the table, she had forced him to acknowledge her - telling him that she recognized him from Nicole's barbecue, asking him about his parents and his job. Sarah had just sat there looking stupid because she had been excluded from the conversation. Then Sarah grabbed Tommy's hand and pulled him to the dance floor. TerriLynn saw the way Sarah was clinging to Tommy when they were slow dancing and the way she had looked at her. Telling TerriLynn with her eyes, *This is my man. You're never going to have him.*

Well, the woman didn't know who she was messing with. TerriLynn glanced around, and then moved to the chair where Tommy had been seated. She opened her purse, found the bottle of sleeping pills that she took occasionally, and took out two pills. The doctor had made a point of telling her to only take *one* at bedtime. She glanced around again, surreptitiously pulled Sarah's drink in front of her, dropped in the pills and watched them dissolve. She looked around one more time, positive that no one had seen her, and then moved back to her seat, smiling to herself and bobbing her head along with the music.

When Sarah and Tommy returned to their seats exhausted and thirsty from dancing, Sarah grabbed her glass and took a long drink, followed by another one. Sarah didn't understand why she suddenly felt so sleepy and somewhat nauseous, too, a short while later. She'd only had two drinks – and had barely finished the second one.

"Are you okay?" Tommy asked.

"I'm just really tired all of a sudden. I had a long day. I might have to call it a night," she said, smiling apologetically. She had really wanted to spend the evening with Tommy.

TerriLynn had disappeared, much to Sarah's delight, and Peter was sitting in her chair. "I was just getting ready to leave," he said. "And I'm going your way. I can drop you off."

Tommy was a bit hesitant. But thought, *Peter and Sarah worked together* and he seemed like a nice guy. He felt that she would be safe with him. But he didn't think it was right for him to stay if Sarah didn't feel well. "I'll take you home," he said.

"No, Sarah," said. "You should stay, Tommy." She knew Tommy was having a good time. There were several people there that he knew and he was also doing some networking. She didn't want to ruin his chance to make some business connections. "Peter's leaving anyway, so he can drop me off." She wrote her address on a napkin and handed it to Peter, "just in case I'm asleep. I'm awfully tired."

Tommy was relieved, and then immediately felt flushed with guilt. But he didn't really want to leave. It had been hard for him to keep his eyes off TerriLynn and his baser instincts had come into play. She looked incredibly hot tonight, even more so than usual. And he couldn't wait to get her alone. He hadn't seen her for a while, but he knew she was still there whenever he wanted her.

"Okay," Tommy said. "I'll call you later." He kissed Sarah's cheek, and then looked at Peter. "Thanks man," he said, shaking his hand. "Take care of my baby."

Peter smiled and nodded, while thinking that *if I had a woman like Sarah, I'd never send her off with another man.*

As Peter was driving, Sarah sat in the passenger seat slumped over. "Sarah are you awake?" he asked.

Sarah didn't respond. She felt totally exhausted and could hardly keep her eyes open. Moments later, she was fast asleep.

Peter parked in front of Sarah's building and woke her up. Sarah was groggy and disoriented and Peter had to practically carry her to the elevator and up to her condo.

Sarah fell straight into bed without taking off her clothes; she didn't even have the strength to undress herself.

Tommy got home pretty late. He had called Sarah from his cell phone before he left with TerriLynn, but she hadn't answered. He figured she was knocked out. Tommy assumed that Sarah had been working really long hours and that it was finally starting to catch up with her. He never would've thought that TerriLynn was capable of doing what she'd done to Sarah. He never would've thought, even in his wildest dreams, that TerriLynn had plans to destroy his relationship with Sarah by any means necessary.

After Tommy fell asleep that night, he started dreaming about a woman who was wearing a red dress. From far away she appeared beautiful, but when he got close to her face, she was the most horrible woman he'd ever seen.

Tommy had been cheating on Sarah with TerriLynn for almost a year now. TerriLynn had always known about Sarah, but Sarah knew nothing about TerriLynn. Tommy knew that if Sarah found out, that would be the end of their relationship, and as much as he loved being with TerriLynn, he did not want his relationship with Sarah to end. He knew that it wasn't right, but all his life, women had always thrown themselves at him. And all his life, he had always found it hard to resist.

Tommy felt like he was in quicksand; slowly sinking between the two women. He knew that he needed to end one of the relationships. He also knew that he loved Sarah, and that what he felt for TerriLynn was simply lust. He knew that the flesh was weak and felt deep down that a physical relationship only truly mattered when it was between two people who loved each other. He did not love TerriLynn; but his physical desire for her was overwhelming. So, he decided to have a talk with his mother.

Tommy was curious about how to deal with women on a spiritual level. Tommy knew about taking a woman out and whining and dining her. He knew how to converse with women and how to listen more than he talked. He knew how to give her the finer things in life because he remembered how much his mother didn't have.

Cindy knew something about how Tommy had treated women in the past. She told him to sit down and handed him a book of prayers (A Man Praying for His Wife, located on the last pages of this book) that could be passed on to the boys and men in the family. When she read the title, she thought that this would be great for the men in her family. When she tried to get Ralph to read it, he said he didn't have time.

Somebody had to break the generational curse that was spreading throughout the family. Somebody had to bring the family to the knowledge of how men were supposed to treat women. It was difficult for Tommy to accept what his mother was trying to teach him. He wasn't ready because he still had several women calling him trying to get with him. He created a world around him that was not true. The life Tommy was living was false and vain.

Tommy took the book that his mother handed him.

"Tommy this is a really good book," Cindy said. "You should read it before you get married and continue to read it while you're married, until it becomes a part of you."

The book listed prayers that teach a man how to pray for his wife.

Tommy called Sarah to let her know that he had decided to go on a week's vacation alone to New York, so that he could get his head straight. Sarah was a bit confused, and she was going to miss him. But she told him that she understood, and that she'd talk to him when he got back.

Tommy made his flight reservation, booked his hotel, and headed out the following week. He took the book that his mother had given him and started reading it on the plane.

The first section started with *I will love her as the weaker vessel.* Tommy was puzzled because he saw Sarah and his mother as strong women. He didn't see women as weaker vessels, so he knew he had a lot to learn about women. The men in his family had never prepared him for the journey he was about to take.

He knew his mother studied the Bible and walked in it because there was no way she could have stayed with his father if it hadn't been for a higher power that had sustained her. Tommy continued reading. The book showed the actual scripture of where it states a woman is a weaker vessel meaning tender and gentle.

The book drew Tommy into it so much that he couldn't put it down. It was so interesting to read prayers that would connect a man to his wife. He never heard the men in his family praying for their wives. This was all new to him; he was totally captivated by the prayers.

The book gave new meaning to marriage. It made him feel that purpose was somehow connected to these prayers. The book also gave him insight on what to pray for. His mother felt just like Solomon's mother when she told him in Proverbs 31 about what kind of woman to look for. Solomon's mother described the woman to be a virtuous woman and then she began to describe what a virtuous woman was.

*   *   *

Sarah had been quickly advanced during her time at Lancing Caruthers & Associates Inc., CPA's; she was now managing her own department. She was a great leader and was able to delegate work without constantly checking behind people. Sarah always waited until the work was almost done to check with her staff to see how they were handling the projects.

Tommy was pulling in clients of big construction companies that were looking for electricians to do the wiring in their construction projects. These projects included high rise buildings, condos and lofts. Tommy was doing well and the years he invested in college were finally paying off. He had to hire a larger staff to keep up.

Because of their busy schedule, Tommy and Sarah spent time eating home cooked meals at their parents' houses. Jeffrey, Sarah's father, didn't like Tommy for some reason. He always gave Tommy a hard time when he came to visit. Sarah tried to convince Tommy to just ignore her father. "That's just his way," she told him. But she couldn't figure out what her father had against Tommy.

On one occasion, Tommy's mother invited him and Sarah to a cookout. The entire family was coming and Cindy wanted them to meet Sarah. She thought Tommy had really made the right choice when he started dating her.

Sarah was starting to wonder if Tommy would ever pop the big question. She was ready to get married from the time she was a little girl playing with her Barbie® doll in the dollhouse with Ken.

After Tommy got situated on the plane, he opened the book. He closed it, looked at the cover and read out loud, "A Man Praying for His Wife." He thought to himself, *Lord, please help me to see in Sarah what you want me to see. I know what I want, but my fleshly desires keep falling back into my old ways.* He opened the book again and started reading it.

Tommy had read the entire book by the time he arrived in New York. He felt that reading it once wasn't enough, so he decided to reread it and meditate on it while he was on vacation. Something had happened to Tommy. It seemed like an intervention had taken place.

That night, after checking into the hotel, Tommy was getting ready for bed when suddenly a bright light appeared in the corner of the room. The light slowly spread across the room, growing progressively brighter, until the entire room was illuminated. In the midst of the light was a man dressed in white with a hood covering his head. There was a rope wrapped around his waist as a belt. Underneath the hood Tommy noticed the man's face was brown with coarse hair hanging down from his head into his face. He was holding his hands out to Tommy as if he were telling him to come.

Tommy was frightened because he had never seen anything like this before. He knew that he needed to start attending church again. When he was a little boy his mother made sure he went with her. Tommy started trembling and the only thing he thought to do was call Sarah. It was kind of late and he hoped that she'd still be awake.

Sarah was still awake. She was staring at the television, but not really watching it. She was thinking about how much she missed Tommy.

Tommy dialed Sarah's number. The phone rang twice, but when Sarah answered, Tommy suddenly was unable to speak.

"Hello," Sarah said. Her greeting was met by the sound of someone breathing. "Hello," she repeated. Is anyone there?"

Tommy tried to speak, but his words seemed to tangle themselves in his throat, and he started coughing.

"Look, stop playing on the phone," Sarah said angrily.

"No, no wait, Sarah. It's me," Tommy finally managed to say.

"Oh! Tommy," Sarah said with excitement. "Hey baby. I'm missing you."

"I'm doing more than missing you. I'm all alone in 'The Big Apple.'" He paused for a moment, thinking about what he had just experienced. "Something unbelievable just happened, Sarah."

"What?"

Tommy went on to tell Sarah what he had experienced and how it made him feel. He said, "I'm afraid. But I know that I should be doing something pertaining to the call on my life for God. Sarah, to be honest, as soon as I get back home, I want to sit down and talk with you about how we need to be together and how we should be in church mingling with the saints. I'll call you as soon as I get back so that we can talk about it. Okay."

"Okay, baby," Sarah said. "I just want you to know that I'm missing you so much. Call me as soon as the plane lands. Sweet dreams."

After Tommy hung up, he fell asleep and started dreaming again. This dream was so real that Tommy was looking at himself, and he was wearing exactly what he wore to bed. *If I am outside than why am I wearing my pajamas?* he thought.

Tommy saw himself trying to climb the stairs to the church that sat on a hill. When he got closer and closer to the church, the stairs got narrower. He almost fell as he climbed higher and higher. When he got almost close to the door, he saw people hanging onto the wall. He asked one man why he was hanging on the wall. The man replied, "I wanted to give my life to Christ, but almost in the door, I thought, why should I? I enjoyed myself while I was in the world."

Tommy said, "Why not just go back down the stairs and finish living your life." The man said, "I remember when I was in the world, although I was having a good time, it didn't benefit me - nothing worked," to which Tommy replied, "Well, come and go with me. I am going in the door." The man said, "I need more time to think about it."

Tommy noticed that when he was on his way in, his bible had fallen out of his arms. He looked back on the stairs and saw it. *My God*, Tommy thought. He went back to get his Bible and found it more difficult to go down the stairs to get it, and once he grabbed it, it was even harder trying to get back up the stairs.

"Why didn't I hold onto my Bible?" Tommy asked himself. I need the Word of God like never before. He eventually got back up the stairs and this time the man hanging on the wall was trying to convince him that serving the Lord is extremely hard and the devil will really be after him. The spiritual battles alone will have you trying to run for cover," the man explained.

The man started telling him the story about Elijah and how he ran from Jezebel. He told him that the woman was so bad that she made a man of God that predicted no rain (I Kings 17:1) question the anointing in his life. Just imagine you trying to give your life to Christ.

Tommy awoke with sweat popping out of every pore on his body. He got out of bed, went into the kitchen of his suite and drank a large glass of water without stopping. What's really going on here? Tommy asked himself. He headed back to bed, fell quickly back to sleep, and the dream continued where it had left off. However, this time he had entered the doors of the church and was walking down a long corridor that led to the main sanctuary. It was amazing. The place was beautiful inside. Tommy thought, if only I could get to the main sanctuary. It seemed as if it was taking a lifetime. He saw several people in the hall that were smiling, and almost to the door of the sanctuary. One man said to Tommy, "Man, you do not want to go in there. It is awful. You will not get what you came for."

Tommy said, "I've come this far; I might as well go in and see what God has for me." He told the man to stop trying to convince people not to surrender their lives to the calling that the Lord has ordained for them.

Tommy kept feeling an urgency in his spirit and a pulling for him to open the door of the sanctuary and go right in. Once he got in the door, he felt he had entered heaven. It was beautiful. The ambience and artifacts gave off an aura of how the glory of the Lord would hover over a room.

All throughout the night, Tommy kept waking up between scenes. This time when he awoke, instead of sweating, he was shivering in a cold sweat. He went into the closet and got a larger blanket. This time, when he fell asleep, his dream took him to the interpretation of it.

The Lord appeared in the middle of the aisle and told Tommy that He summons him to come so that He could deal with a personal matter with Tommy. The Lord sat Tommy on one of the pews and began to tell him what happened when he first started dreaming.

I called you out from where you were and you decided to come. The stairs represent how far away your interest toward Me was. As you climbed the stairs, the smaller they became, showed how difficult you were making it within yourself of getting closer to Me. Your perseverance and tenacity gave you strength to keep coming. When you dropped your Bible on the stairs that represented how important the Word of God was to you. You hardly read your Word and you keep making excuses as to why you don't want to mingle with the saints. The man you saw hanging on the wall not wanting to go into the church represented the people you used to hang out with. They wanted to go to church and have a relationship with Me, but they decided to only give Me part of their heart. Remember, you have to be either cold or hot; otherwise, I will spew you out of My mouth. When you went back to get your Bible, I noticed your effort and gave you the ability to get it and climb back up to get inside the church. Keep in mind, that you are the church not this building made up of bricks. Once you got inside, I felt the thirst you had after righteousness. Then I knew, Tommy that you were really ready to get to know Me more, corporately. The man standing outside the door trying to convince you not to go in was another representation of people you were hanging around, influencing you through your ear gate of what you should do. You really let the men in your family affect some of your decisions and choices you made in life. I watched you over the years and knew the bad choices you made. I still kept knocking at the door of your heart waiting for you to open it. You wouldn't listen to Me during the day, so I would give you dreams in the night season hoping that you would listen to Me. You've made my heart glad to see you've made it into the sanctuary, but don't let that be the last thing you do. It is up to you to work out your own salvation with fear and trembling. Tommy you have to pass salvation and accept the call on your life. Don't let time go by because the enemy's desire is to sift you like wheat. I've charged legions of angels to encamp around you to fight for you if you want them to. They will only move when you call on Me and speak positive words out of your mouth. When you speak negatively, that stops the angels from activating greatness around you.

Enjoy the service today because this is the day that you will join this ministry, and give your heart wholeheartedly to Me. My eyes are watching you and My ears are attentive to every word you speak out of your mouth. Bless you, Tommy. I will be with you always even until the ends of the world.

Tommy got up the following morning and prepared for his 2:00 p.m. flight. He made sure he had enough time to pack, shower, eat breakfast, and get to the airport.

While on the way to the airport, his phone rang; it was Sarah.

"Hello," Tommy said.

"It's me," Sarah said. "How are you?"

"I'm on my way to the airport. I'll call you as soon as I land."

"Do you want me to pick you up from the airport?"

"Thanks for asking," Tommy said. "But I need to take care of some things first before I stop by this evening. I'll see you later."

"Okay," Sarah said. "I'll wait to hear from you. Have a safe trip."

"Okay," Tommy said. "I can't wait to see you and tell you about my experience. Bye, baby."

Tommy boarded the plane and sat in an aisle seat close to the front. He wanted to be the first one off the plane. The weather was rainy so the plane experienced a lot of turbulence. Tommy grabbed the arms attached to his seat, closed his eyes, and started praying to God. He took out his MP3 player and plugged the ear plugs into his ears. He sat back and fell asleep. When he opened his eyes the plane had landed. He stretched and stood up to get his luggage. He noticed that most of the passengers had already left the plane.

Tommy was extremely tired because while he was trying to sleep in New York, the Lord was dealing with him. He caught a cab home to drop off his luggage, check on his mail, and make sure his loft was still intact.

Sarah couldn't wait to see Tommy. She had cleaned her condo so well that there wasn't a pinch of dust to be seen. For dinner, she ordered steak, lobster tails, two loaded baked potatoes, and a salad with all the toppings. She had a bottle of fine merlot on ice. Candles were set on the table and around her place. The aroma of Glade® Clean Linen filled the air. She had soft music playing, Kenny G, because she loved how his music set the mood in her place. The phone rang. Tommy hadn't called Sarah to let her know he was on his way. He decided to stop by because he really missed her.

It was the doorman, "Tommy is here to see you," he said. Excited and somewhat nervous, Sarah told him to send Tommy up.

Tommy got on the elevator and when the elevator stopped, beautiful young women got on discussing their plans for the evening. They were going up to pick up another friend for a night out on the town. Tommy loved going out, so he asked where they were going. One young lady said, "We're going to The Caplan's on Main Street." The Caplan's was the place where all nationalities came together to party. The DJs on all 3 levels were trained in the art of mixing all types of music - Jazz, House, Reggae or R&B/Hip Hop.

The young ladies got off the elevator and Tommy told them to have a good time. Tommy thought to himself, I can take Sarah out to The Caplan's sometimes. What

Tommy didn't know was that Sarah had already been to The Caplan's, which is where she had met Peter.

Sarah opened the door right before Tommy knocked. "Hello, handsome," she said, with a wide smile.

Tommy returned Sarah's smile. "Hey, gorgeous." He kissed her on the cheek. "It smells good in here." He walked into the living room. What is that fragrance?"

"It's a mixture of things," Sarah said. "It could be what I've prepared for dinner, and it could be the fragrance that you like.

Tommy smiled and sniffed, "Clean Linen?"

"Yes," Sarah said, smiling.

The table was already set and Sarah thought it would be nice to eat first and then maybe look at a movie or play dominos. Sarah loved numbers, so dominos was what she enjoyed playing. She started the meal with a light salad and then a small bowl of vegetable soup. The bread was delicious, and she had softened butter with honey for them to use as a spread. When it was time to serve the main course, Tommy stared at Sarah for a long moment before he spoke. "Sarah," he said, "You are really good to me. You know my heart and you've shown me that you are the woman for me."

Sarah smiled and looked into Tommy's eyes, which appeared to be sparkling. "Tommy what happened in New York? You look even better than you did before you left. Heck, I need to go to New York."

Tommy laughed. "It wasn't New York. It was the Lord. He kept talking to me and dealing with me."

Sarah stared at Tommy with a curious expression. "The Lord?"

Tommy nodded.

"What are you trying to tell me, Tommy?"

Tommy said, "The Lord was clearly explaining to me my life and how it was going and what I need to do to get it together. Sarah, I want to move forward with my life and not continue being stuck in this place where I am."

Sarah misunderstood what Tommy was saying. "Move forward?" What are you saying?" Her voice was filled with a mild panic. She thought Tommy was saying that he wanted to move forward *without* her.

"No, no," Tommy said quickly. "Don't take me the wrong way. I want to tell you something, and I think this is the right time."

Sarah stared at Tommy; she was excited, but also confused.

"Let's finish our dinner," Tommy said. "Then we can talk about it."

"Okay," Sarah said forcing a smile, although she was impatient to hear what Tommy had to tell her.

Sarah thought she knew pretty much what Tommy wanted to say because she felt the same way. Sarah felt that they were connected spiritually, physically and mentally. The physical connection was not about sex because Tommy wanted it to be right with Sarah. He knew that sexual desires that were defiled could lead to sexual misconduct. They exercised together at times, which helped them to learn one another's physical stamina. As Tommy was eating his lobster tail, he kept saying, "Ummm this is delicious. I'm so glad you can cook, baby."

Sarah looked over at him and winked her right eye as if saying, *I've got you now.*

After dinner, they decided to snuggle on the couch and watch a good movie. When Tommy turned on the television, a news flash came on stating that a bad thunderstorm was heading to the area, and that those who were indoors should stay inside. Tommy thought this was great; *I can stay here with Sarah all night. I know she missed me as much as I missed her*, he thought.

Sarah looked at Tommy as if she had read his mind, "I missed you Tommy, and it would be nice if we spent tonight together."

Tommy smiled. "Sarah, I've been thinking about us, and I want to take our relationship to the next level."

"The next level?" Sarah asked. "Tommy, what are you saying?"

He said, "When I'm home by myself, I can't get you off my mind. I try, but your face keeps appearing and then my heart starts beating fast."

Sarah said, "Tommy, I hope you know what you're saying. My feelings are at stake, and I can really give my heart to you. I've been in bad relationships in my past. I guess I'm sort of afraid to move to the next level."

"You have to face your fear Sarah," Tommy said gently.

"I know," Sarah said. "I just don't want to get my heart broken."

"You never have to worry about me hurting you, Sarah. If I say I'm ready, then I am."

"Well, you know I love you, Tommy. You make me feel like a special kind of woman. You give me the confidence I need to go throughout the day knowing that I have a good man by my side."

"You've given of yourself many times and you didn't know that I felt like a king."

"A king?"

"Yes, a king."

"Look at you. You're already making me feel like I've accomplished something great."

"I meant to do that. I want you to know that you helped me get to where I am. I believe I couldn't have gotten this far without you."

"Tommy, we've known each other for over a year now."

"I know, during the short time we've been together I've accomplished so much."

"Well, baby, ask me."

"Ask you what?"

Sarah turned to look at Tommy as if she was going to punch him out. He grabbed her and started laughing.

"Baby, would you marry me?"

"Yes, Yes, Yes, Yes, Yes."

Tommy pulled her close and they kissed for at least 10 minutes. Love was in the air and Sarah was ready to really take their relationship to the next level.

Tommy said, "Sarah we've waited all this time. We might as well wait until our big day. I want this relationship to be right. I want it to be different from all my other relationships."

Sarah said, "Let's look at this movie and get some rest. We have a lot of planning to do and this will give us more time to spend together."

Tommy said, "Yes, this will be our test to see if we can stand to be together and to handle business arrangements."

"Business arrangements?"

"Why do you ask so many questions, Sarah?"

"I was just wondering what business."

"Marriage is really a business between two people that set goals to reach, so that the business of marriage will not lack and have to do without our necessities."

You realize that what we do already can be put together to accomplish more. Your business classes in school will come in handy," Sarah said.

"Yeah, now you see what I am saying."

"Tommy, that's why I love you. You are truly a leader that's going to help us get to where we're going."

"Do you really know where we're going?"

"No, but as long as I get there with you, I'll be fine," Sarah said.

"Sarah, when we finally do the Damn thing, I want to make you the happiest woman in the world."

"Oh, Tommy."

"Come here woman. Sit as close to me as you can because I'm not letting you out of my sight for the rest of the evening."

"Okay. Whatever you say," Sarah said, smiling.

"I want to propose to you in front of our parents and then when you say, yes, I'll put your engagement ring on your finger. I want your father to see how happy you are, and I want to ask him for his daughter's hand in marriage."

That night Sarah and Tommy fell asleep on the couch while the movie was watching them. They snuggled together comfortably until Sarah was awakened by the ringing of the telephone.

"Hello"

"Hello, Sarah. This is mom."

"Hi mom. How are you?"

"I'm fine. Just calling to check on you to see if you were inside. It's raining pretty badly."

"I saw the weather report and the raindrops are hitting my windows pretty hard." And then she got really quiet. Sarah didn't want to imply to her mother that Tommy was there, so she tried to get her off the phone. She really couldn't wait to *spill the beans* and let her mother know that she had been asked the big question.

"Call me in the morning, dear."

"I will. Have a good night, mom."

"Okay, baby. I will."

They just hung up the phone because they never really wanted to say goodbye. Sarah's mother thought goodbye meant you would never see the person again. Her mother wanted to keep Sarah a little girl and when Sarah moved out to go to college, her mother got pretty emotional and started crying.

Sarah and Tommy got off the couch and climbed into bed together. As Tommy promised, nothing happened. He really wanted this time to be different. Sarah pulled back the covers and asked him, "Which side of the bed do you sleep on?"

"I sleep all over the bed, but I'll sleep on the side close to the window."

"Cool. Because I like to sleep near the door."

Tommy kissed Sarah on her forehead and said, "sleep tight."

When they finally got situated in bed together, Tommy fell asleep first and started dreaming. He saw a woman in a red dress calling him to come to her. He tried very hard in the dream not to come. She was really beautiful, so it was quite difficult for Tommy to resist. She was moving her body in such a way that kept getting his attention until finally he started running toward her. When he reached her, he looked right in her face and saw scales and wrinkles. From a distance, she looked beautiful, but when he got up close, the truth was revealed. He started screaming as if he'd seen a ghost and awakened Sarah.

"Tommy, what's wrong?" Sarah said, her voice laced with concern. "Why are you screaming? Are you having another nightmare?"

"Yes, and I really need to seek God concerning what that was all about. This is the second time I've had this dream."

Sarah said, "Do you want to talk about it?"

"No," Tommy said.

Sarah said, "Let me get you something to drink, so that we can get some sleep."

"Thank you, baby."

Sarah went to the kitchen, and Tommy looked up at the ceiling and asked God, "Are you trying to tell me something about my engagement?" He waited to hear something from God. He couldn't hear God saying anything.

"Tommy here's your water. This should help you sleep."

Tommy reached for the glass and finished it in one gulp.

"You must have been thirsty. Maybe it was the lobster you ate that gave you that bad dream."

"I'm not sure what it was. I'm really tired. Let's try to go back to sleep."

"Baby, have a good night."

Before they knew it, it was Sunday morning. Sarah was still basking in the thought that she was going to be Mrs. Tommy Whitfield.

Tommy pulled into the driveway of his parents' house. He got out of the car, walked to the sidewalk and looked down the street. He noticed the block was really quiet. He rang the doorbell although he still had a key. He didn't want to barge in. His mother answered the door.

"Hey, honey. What brings you to this neighborhood?"

"I stopped by to tell you and dad something very important."

"Important?"

"Yeah. Where's dad?"

"He's out back working in the yard."

"Let me go and talk with him first."

Tommy walked through the house out the back door and yelled, "Hey dad."

His father walked over to him. "It's good to see you, son. What's going on?"

"I just stopped by to talk to you and mom about something very important that will change my life. Before I do, I want to ask you something. When I was a little boy, why did you and Uncle Ralph talk about all those women you had over the years?"

"Tommy, we didn't mean anything by it. We were just shooting the breeze and talking about nothing."

"Well dad, I was listening and thought that women were only sex objects. I thought that I was supposed to put notches in my belt, too. I didn't realize who women really were."

"Well son, let me tell you from my perspective. Women are God's gift to God's green earth. They are the prize that we go after to win. We are hunters and we have to prey on them and go after them until we catch our prey. A man that finds a wife, finds a good thing and obtains favor from the Lord. (Emphasis added - Proverbs 18:22)

"When you go around from woman to woman, your life seems unstable, although it feels good for a short time. Then you realize as you get older what's really important in life. Son, don't get me wrong. Over the years I had fun and lived my life, but I had to come to a conclusion that I'm going to get old, and I wanted someone in my life who can grow with me.

"Your mother is the type of woman that takes her hands and builds up her house. She keeps me healthy and stayed with me when I didn't know how to treat her. Are you listening, son?"

"Yes, I'm listening. Dad, I'm so glad that I was able to talk to you. It always seemed as if we were too busy to sit down and have this conversation. I'm glad we did before I take this big step."

"What big step?"

"Let's go into the house so that I can tell you and mom together."

"Okay. Let me clean my hands as he wiped his hands on an old white towel. Your mom would scream if I bring this dirt into the house."

"I know. When I was little, she would always say that she needed to hose me down before I come into the house." Tommy laughed at the memory.

They proceeded into the house and found Cindy sleeping on the couch. He didn't realize that he and his father had spent so much time in the backyard talking. Tommy said, "Mom, mom wakeup. I've got something to tell you."

"Oh, baby. I didn't realize I'd fallen asleep."

"Dad, mom listen. I want to marry Sarah. She's really a good woman for me. Mom, doesn't the Bible say that a man that finds a wife finds a good thing and obtains favor from the Lord?" (Emphasis added)

Cindy said, "Yes."

Tommy said, "I want my favor. I need the favor of God on my life. Sarah is a lovely young lady, and she knows how to love me."

Ralph asked, "Are you sure?"

"Yes dad. I'm sure. I've really thought this through. I didn't want to jump into this and not be sure. I'm tired of living a life of being with this woman and that woman. It's time I grow up and settle down. Can we have a barbecue and invite her parents so that I can ask Sarah's father for his daughter?"

Ralph and Cindy looked at each other and smiled.

Ralph said, "This is great. Our son is getting married. I'm so proud of him."

Tommy really liked to hear his dad confirm his decision. He agreed that Sarah was a nice young lady, and Tommy couldn't have picked a better woman to be his wife.

Tommy called Sarah to tell her that he was stopping by. "I'll see you in about an hour," he said.

Sarah cooked pot roast in her slow cooker, with potatoes, carrots, celery, corn, and had smothered it in beef gravy. She made a light salad to eat before the main dish. Her mom gave her a recipe to make homemade dinner rolls. They were delicious and melted in your mouth.

When Tommy arrived, he noticed Sarah was busy doing a number of things, so he asked her, "Can you stop moving around and come and sit next to me?" Sarah was nervous, but stopped what she was doing, walked over and sat down next to Tommy. "Do you want something to drink," she asked.

Tommy said, "sure."

Sarah rose to go and get the bottle of wine from the *fridge*.

Tommy said, "No, I'll get it. I need to learn how to maneuver in your place." Sarah sat back and allowed Tommy to serve her. They decided to watch the movie *I Am Legend* directed by Francis Lawrence starring Will Smith. Tommy felt that Will had similar features and he admired how he carried himself. Sarah kinda sorta looked like Will's wife Jada.

After pouring the drinks, Tommy handed Sarah her glass of wine. He picked his up and said, "let's toast to a life together forever."

They both sat back on the coach. Tommy pressed the remote to start the movie. Sarah was enjoying this. She was really happy. She leaned over and kissed him. Tommy grabbed her and started kissing Sarah as if he had been waiting on this opportunity. He didn't want to rush things, but when the opportunity presented itself, Tommy knew that he was going to take charge.

The movie was still playing and they really got beside themselves. Sarah didn't want it to go any further, so she pulled back and said, "Wait. Let's eat dinner and get back to watching the movie."

Tommy said, "Alright."

They walked over to the dinner table and Tommy pulled his chair out and sat down. Sarah uncovered their salads and placed them on the table. When she got close to Tommy, he grabbed the back of her thigh and squeezed it hard enough to let Sarah know he wasn't finished with her.

After dinner, they both sat back on the couch to finish watching the movie. Tommy really wanted to wait for any intimacy and wanted to be sure Sarah was willing to wait. He didn't want this relationship to end up like the others, so he was trying to do things differently.

Once the movie went off, Tommy told Sarah that he had a great time, and he'd see her soon. Because both of them had to get up in the morning, they decided to call it a night. Sarah walked Tommy to the door and they kissed goodbye. It was awesome because Sarah made Tommy feel like he was the man because Sarah agreed with everything he said.

Sarah slept like a baby that night knowing that she had someone in her life that loved her and respected her feelings. She got up that morning singing and humming a melody throughout the house. She drove in to work playing her favorite song over and over again.

She parked her car in the garage. While riding the elevator up to her office, she ran into one of her girlfriends who told her about this big event that was coming up. She told Sarah she'd send her an invitation for her and a guest.

When Sarah walked into the office, she noticed a large arrangement of flowers. She asked the receptionist if they were for her. The receptionist smiled and said, "They sure are." Sarah was sure they were from Tommy.

A while into Sarah and Tommy's relationship, Sarah had started receiving flowers at work. The company where she worked had her name listed on their website, so it was public information. The flowers started coming in at least once a week; sometimes twice a week. The note would always say, "Hi, sweetie. I can't wait to see you. Hopefully, soon. Yours truly, xox." Sarah was puzzled. *Why would someone send flowers and not say who they were?*

Since the cards were never signed, Sarah didn't mention to Tommy that she'd been receiving flowers. Tommy noticed Sarah was not as friendly and open with him as before. She pulled back from him several times. Tommy wondered what was wrong. Everything was going along fine and suddenly the relationship had come to a hard place. This was a challenge for him. Men are hunters. Here was an opportunity for Tommy to start hunting to find out why Sarah started changing after he proposed to her. Sarah started getting nervous about a committed relationship. She knew this was what she wanted, but was having second thoughts.

One night when Tommy was over, Sarah's phone rang. "Hi Sarah. This is Peter. How are you doing?" One of Sarah's acquaintances gave Peter her cell phone number. He was charming and knew how to get what he wanted.

"I'm fine," Sarah said. "How did you get my number?"

"I got it from a friend of yours. I hope you don't mind."

"No. It's okay," Sarah said. She'd had a really good time that night with Peter at The Caplan's.

Peter asked, "What are you doing this weekend?"

Sarah said, "Let me check my schedule, and I'll get back to you. Okay?"

Peter said, "That's fine. Let me give you my phone number." He gave Sarah his phone number and she told him that she would call. She didn't write it down because Tommy was there. Also, she had caller ID.

Tommy said, "Business?"

Sarah nodded, feeling a flicker of guilt about being untruthful.

"I heard of The Caplan's," Tommy said. "I wanted to take you there. But I see you've already been." Tommy sounded a bit disappointed.

"It's a nice place," Sarah said. "We should go there some time."

PLANNING THE WEDDING CEREMONY

Tommy and Sarah had been engaged for three months and decided it was time to start planning their wedding. Sarah was excited about getting a wedding planner, while Tommy didn't care what plans Sarah made. He wanted to be sure that the honeymoon was in a secluded place where it was just the two of them. He got several brochures to different romantic vacation spots to show Sarah so they could narrow it down to two places.

Sarah started looking up wedding planners on-line and found some that would create scenarios of other countries. She thought that would be really something to have a wedding and bring Paris, Singapore, or the Bahamas to their wedding. This way their families and friends could have an experience they would never forget.

Sarah picked up her phone and dialed the first wedding planner that was listed.

"Hello, this is Tania White speaking."

"Hi Tania, this is Sarah Copeland."

"Hi, Sarah," Tania said cheerfully. "What can I help you with?"

"I saw your ad on-line and was wondering if you'd be available to assist me and my fiancé in planning our wedding?"

"How much time do we have?" Tania asked.

Sarah said, "We have three months to plan and we believe the end of summer would be a good time."

"There's a lot to do in three months," Tania said. "Believe it or not, you called me at a good time. I just finished a wedding last week, and it was fabulous."

"I'm so happy to hear that you have time for me and Tommy Whitfield."

Tania asked, "Tommy? That wouldn't happen to be Tommy Whitfield who went to Kaplan College, who owns his own electrical business?

Small world, Sarah thought. "That's right. That's my Tommy."

"It's so nice to hear that he's tying the knot with you. When Tommy and I were in college, I always thought he had so much potential, and I kept telling him to get his act together."

Sarah laughed. "I'm glad someone told him. When he was in college, we really didn't know one another. We met one time when we were younger and hadn't seen each other until we both were finished with school."

"Well, I'm happy to hear that the two of you are getting married, and again, I'd love to help you organize it. Let's meet Friday at 2:30 p.m. Stop by my office at the Southwest location. I have two offices so that I can cater to people on both sides of town. Also email me your address so that I can send you a copy of my book, *'So, You're Engaged? An Inspirational Wedding Guide.'* This book has helped many of my customers. I also do meetings with both parties so that I can get a feel of what they both want."

"Sounds good," Sarah said. "I'll see you then."

After hanging up with Tania, Sarah was filled with excitement. Everything seemed to be falling into place. Having a wedding planner would make things move along a lot smoother. She knew Tommy would be happy to know that the wedding planner was someone he knew. She thought she would go to the first meeting alone and then take Tommy to the next scheduled meeting, but she wouldn't tell him who the wedding planner was. She wanted to see the surprise on his face when he saw her.

Tania was a well known planner that not only did weddings, but she also coordinated other events that consisted of thousands of people from upscale to lower class. Tania knew how to take a small amount of money and stretch it to make it look as if she spent millions. She had gone to college and got a Masters in Business. Her books were well organized, and it showed in her outstanding performance. She organized a lot of VIP parties for Hollywood movie stars. She was well versed and well known for her work. After reading about Tania on-line and speaking with her, Sarah knew she had made the right choice.

*   *   *

Sarah pulled up in front of her parents' house. She quickly got out of her car and ran inside, "Mom. Where are you?" she called.

"I'm in the kitchen, honey. What's going on?"

Sarah ran into the kitchen. "Mom," she said excitedly. "It's finally happening." Sarah was jumping up and down, raising her hands in the air, and crying all at the same time. "Mom, I'm getting married. And I'm so happy."

Karen grabbed her daughter, hugged her and started crying, too. Jeffrey ran into the kitchen and seeing both women in tears said, "What's going on? What happened?"

Sarah said, "I'm sorry daddy for all the noise, but I'm getting married."

"Are you marrying that Tommy guy?" dad asked.

"Yes, yes. I am marrying Mr. Tommy Whitfield," Sarah stated proudly.

Jeffrey said, "Baby, I need to talk to you and ask you some important questions. Marriage is no joke, and you really must be serious about this big decision you're making. Sarah, you will always be my little girl, and I'm not going to pass you on to just any man."

Sarah smiled affectionately at her father.

"When will I get a chance to talk to Tommy and then the both of you about this?"

Sarah said, "We'll stop by this weekend. Mom, can you fix dinner for us?"

"Sure, honey," mom said.

71

"I'll do something much better," said Jeffrey. I'll fry some fish and turkey in the deep fryers, and your mom can make the side dishes and her delicious homemade dinner rolls. Invite Tommy and his parents, and we'll make this a family affair. Okay, baby?"

"That sounds great," Sarah said. "We'll be one big happy family."

"Mom, this book came in from the Wedding Planner and it's really beautiful. Take a look," Sarah said.

Her mother took the book and glanced through it. "Oh this is beautiful. Where did you find this Wedding Planner?"

"I found her online. Her website is amazing."

After spending an hour or so with her parents, Sarah went home to catch up on some work.

Sarah called Tommy the moment she got home to tell him about the dinner at her parents' house. When Tommy answered, she was so excited that she started talking without even saying hello.

"Tommy, I want to invite you and your parents over to my parents' house for a fish and turkey fry."

Tommy laughed. "I was going to invite you and your parents to my parent's house for a barbecue. Here we are thinking alike already."

"You know what they say about great minds," Sarah said.

"I tell you what," Tommy said. "We'll go to your parents' house first, and have something at my parents house a week or two later."

Sarah thought this was a great idea. "Okay," she said. "I'll talk with you later."

TWO DAYS LATER

When Sarah arrived at Tania's office, Tania had already made a pot of Chamomile tea. Tania experienced customers that were really nervous and stressed out, so she wanted to begin their meeting with something that would help them relax. The ambience of Tania's office was soft and inviting. The color scheme was purple and lilac with butter yellow colors designed on two opposite walls. The office was spacious as if Tania had just moved in. Tania didn't like a lot of clutter, either physical or mental. She needed to have a clear mind and felt the same about her surroundings.

Tania pulled out a list of questions to ask Sarah. The list consisted of some important and not so important questions. But Tania thought that all the questions were necessary in order to determine exactly what Sarah wanted.

What is the date of the wedding?

"September 7th. On a Saturday early afternoon."

Have you met with your pastor for counseling?

"Tommy and I haven't been to church in a long time, but we can call the church to schedule a meeting with the pastor, as early as next week."

"What theme did you want to go with?"

Tania showed Sarah a portfolio of some of the other themes of events. As Sarah was flipping through the photos, she stopped at one that caught her eye. It looked lovely, and Sarah told Tania that she would have to run it by Tommy first.

Can you bring him to our next meeting?" Tania asked.

"Sure," Sarah said. She'd been thinking about bringing him to the second meeting anyway.

Tania showed Sarah different designs of invitations that would be nice to send out to the guests so their minds would envision the kind of wedding they'd be attending. Tania thought it was good to have the guests looking forward to the ceremony.

"Catering service is very important because if the food and service isn't good, then that makes everything else seem out of place," Tania said.

This was all kind of overwhelming to Sarah. Tania noticed this and suggested they take a break and walk outside on the terrace. The landscaping was beautiful and always seemed to help Tania's customers with their imagination. Their minds would shift from one gear to another.

"This is really nice," Sarah said, looking around.

"Thanks," Tania said, smiling. "Would you like some tea?"

Sarah said, "Sure. Thanks."

"While I go get the tea, look at this other portfolio of banquet halls and see which one would be best for your reception."

Tania walked into the office and graciously returned with a canister of tea. As she poured, she told Sarah about the Limo service. "They'll pick you and your wedding party up then take you to the fitting room at the church. After dropping you off, the Limo then will go and pick up Tommy and the members of his wedding party."

Tania also told Sarah how they helped organize the flights, hotel stay, spas and dining reservations at honeymoon spots. "We also include different activities that take place while honeymooning to keep it a memorable occasion," she said.

This was great because Sarah knew that Tommy had already picked up some brochures for them to look over before deciding which spot would be great. Sarah's happiness and excitement grew as she discussed her wedding plans with Tania.

THE FAMILY FISH AND TURKEY FRY:

Tommy gave his parents the address to Sarah's parents' house. Sarah and Tommy decided to go in the same car and meet his parents there.

Karen and Jeffrey had the place looking and smelling good. They wanted Cindy and Ralph to see they would be great in-laws.

Jeffrey greeted them at the door while Karen was in the kitchen working on the side dishes. Jeffrey had the turkey already in the deep fryer in the backyard. He was going to wait to fry the fish because he wanted it to be hot when he served it. He was happy that his daughter was finally getting married, but had second thoughts about Tommy.

Everyone came in and Sarah asked where her mother was.

"She's in the kitchen," Jeffrey said.

Sarah took her future mother-in-law into the kitchen to meet her mother.

When Sarah and Cindy entered the kitchen, Karen was crying. Sarah quickly walked over to her. "Why are you crying, mom?" she asked, concern in her voice.

"I'm crying because my baby girl is getting married, and I started remembering some of the things I went through. These are tears of joy, sweetheart, but also tears of concern."

Cindy said, "I already shed my tears for both Tommy and Sarah. I hope they realize what they're getting themselves into. When you get married, you do it till death."

"Yes," Karen said. "You have to stick together no matter what. You have to stay focused on what is important and look over the stupid stuff."

Sarah asked, "Stupid stuff?"

Karen said, "Yes, things that don't really matter, but if you put any emphasis on them, they can get blown way out of proportion."

"In order to have a successful marriage, you'll have to look over the minor things, although small things can turn into big ones, and pay attention to what you're trying to accomplish with one another. There are going to be situations that happen to make you want to give up, but you can't," Cindy added.

Sarah said, "Tommy and I have already been through a number of things."

Those things were nursery rhymes compared to what you'll have to deal with once you're married," Cindy said. - *Pattycake, Pattycake, Baker's Man (*Mother Goose Lyric)*. Once you say, *I do*, a lot of things are going to happen to make you want to run and never look back."

Karen nodded "Yeah, honey. You have to be sure that this is what you really want to do for better or for worse."

Sarah stared at the two women, digesting what they'd said.

In the meantime, the men were in the backyard checking on the turkey and drinking beer. Jeffrey had a big screen TV in the yard because there was a basketball game on. The men sat around the TV shouting at the players and the referee as if they could hear them. They were having a good time. Then suddenly, Jeffrey looked at Tommy and asked, "What do you plan on doing with Sarah?"

Tommy was somewhat taken aback by the question. "I plan on keeping her and protecting her. We have great dreams and would like to accomplish them before we let you guys know about them. I love your daughter, and I came over to ask for her hand in marriage." Tommy explained, proud of the way he'd answered her father's question.

Jeffrey asked, "What do you have to offer her?"

"I have a lot to offer your daughter," Tommy said. "I own my own business. I buy property, fix them up, sell them, and make a substantial profit from them.

"Did you see how the housing market is going?" Jeffrey asked.

"What are you going to do when it gets worse?" Jeffrey said.

"We've saved up a lot of money for slow periods in our lives. We saved enough to carry us for at least 10 years."

Jeffrey was impressed. But he still wasn't sure if he was ready to let his "little girl" go, and he expressed that to Tommy.

Ralph interrupted. "Jeffrey, you have to realize that there comes a time when you have to let go. She can't stay a little girl forever."

Jeffrey nodded slowly. "You're right. I'm just not sure if Tommy is the right man for Sarah."

Ralph said, "Jeffrey, they're adults. And we need to let them make their own decisions."

The women came out to the backyard just in time and the conversation ended. Sarah brought out a pitcher of margaritas and poured the men drinks. Cindy and Karen carried the side dishes and the dinner rolls. Jeffrey had already finished frying the fish and had taken the turkey out of the deep fryer. Ralph asked if he could cut the turkey.

"Sure," Jeffrey said, picking up the knife with a towel and handing it to Ralph with the handle first.

When they were almost done eating, Tommy decided to propose to Sarah in front of their parents while everyone was holding their drinks.

Tommy kneeled on one knee while Sarah stood in front of him. He said, "Sarah, I love you so much that I want to be with you for the rest of my life. I don't think that I can live without you. Will you marry me?"

Sarah shouted, "YES!!!" smiling and tearing up. "Tommy," she said, "we won't ever let anything come between us."

Their parents turned to one another happily, while Sarah's father looked puzzled.

Karen and Jeffrey had gone out of their way to be sure this was really nice. Cindy commented that Karen and Jeffrey were excellent cooks. They all sat back, relaxed, watched the game, and enjoyed one another's company.

When Ralph and Cindy were leaving, they decided that they'd get together again soon, but at Cindy and Ralph's next time. Ralph said, "Yeah, we'll do it at my house in a couple of weeks. I'll barbecue before the weather starts changing."

"Sounds great," Jeffrey said.

Cindy stood up to give Karen a hug and said in her ear, "It was nice. I'm looking forward to us being a family."

Karen smiled, "Me too."

Karen and Jeffrey walked them to the door and everyone hugged, shook hands, and said, "See you later." Those were Karen's favorite words. She never wanted to say good-bye.

*   *   *

After the cookout at her parents' house, Tommy and Sarah's relationship took a turn down on an unexpected road. Sarah found herself thinking about Peter. She really didn't understand why because she knew that she loved Tommy. But she admired the way Peter carried himself and he had been such a gentleman when he'd dropped her off that night.

Sarah had gone through Tommy's cell phone and found that TerriLynn had been calling him more than anyone else. When she questioned Tommy about it, he said they were just friends. Sarah knew better because friends don't call each other all day. Heck, she and Tommy only talked once or twice a day. Suddenly, Sarah realized that she'd never gone over to Tommy's bachelor pad. He always came over to her house or they went to one of their parents' houses. When she asked him about visiting his place, he always came up with an excuse - which Sarah had accepted – or he changed the subject. She'd also noticed that lately Tommy didn't call her back when he said he would, and a few times he'd said he was coming over, but would call at the last minute to say he couldn't make it.

Sarah thought that Tommy's behavior was suspicious. She was also angry, hurt and confused. Well, she thought to herself, if Tommy could have a "friend," so could she.

Sarah had touched base with Peter and had planned to go out of town with him. Peter wanted to get away and thought it would be nice to spend that time with Sarah. They went to a secluded place that wasn't too far from the city. Sarah was apprehensive about going to a secluded place with Peter because she didn't know him that well, but for some reason, she trusted him. What she did know about Peter was that he owned a beauty salon/spa, which was very successful. He was well known throughout Ohio and other states.

His salon was called "Salon Beauté (beauty salon)." The barbers' room was called "salon de coiffure (barber shop)." The juice bar was in a room off to the side; it served coffee, tea and all sorts of juice drinks and was called "salon de thé (tea room)." The foyer where the waiting clients sat was called "salon de devant (en façade) which means front room." He also had hair stylists for children that focused on developing children in the area of reading and math while they waited. This was a family oriented salon. His shop had a spa area and an area for Nail Technicians. Right next door from the shop was a restaurant that served healthy food. Peter wanted to service people from the inside out.

Peter loved to swim and Sarah loved to exercise, so they both decided to spend time in the exercise room where the pool was located in a separate area. They were able to relax and enjoy one another's company and discuss some business transactions. Peter had a great accountant, but wanted some of Sarah's expertise. Peter believed in bringing out the best in women.

Sarah's phone rang while they were going up to the room. She looked at her phone and decided not to answer it.

"You should answer it," Peter said. "It could be important."

Sarah shook her head. "I'll call them back later." When the elevator door opened, Peter extended his hand to let Sarah go out first. *He is such a gentleman,* Sarah thought. Then another thought entered Sarah's mind. *Why am I enjoying myself so much with another man during a time when I should be making one of the most important decisions of my life?* Isn't that how the enemy works?

Peter didn't want to take advantage or be intimate with Sarah; he just wanted to spend a weekend together. Some women think men want to be intimate with them as soon as possible. But that is not always the case. There are some men who really want to wait before joining themselves to a woman. Peter wanted to spend some time away and enjoy life with no commitment.

Believe it or not, Sarah wanted to save herself for Tommy when they got married. She still wanted to marry him; she just wanted to see if this weekend with Peter would change her mind. Well, it didn't. She still felt Tommy in her spirit. Sarah was missing him.

Tommy didn't know where Sarah was and this really put something on his mind. He was feeling lonely and stayed near the phone just in case she called. He kept checking his cell phone to see if he'd missed her call. He knew about the meeting she'd scheduled with Tania, the Wedding Coordinator. After that meeting, Tommy and Sarah were going to start rehearsal for the wedding ceremony.

The next day Tommy still hadn't heard from Sarah. He was really worried about her. He decided to seek his mother's advice. He didn't want to let Karen and Jeffrey know because considering the way Jeffrey felt about him, he might think that Tommy had done something to Sarah.

Tommy was really nervous by the time his mother answered the phone. "Mom, this is Tommy, I need your help."

"Of course, Tommy. What is it?"

"I can't find Sarah," he said. "She's been gone for a couple of days and she's not answering her phone."

"Did you and Sarah have an argument?"

"Kind of, sort of. She checked my cell phone and noticed that a girl had been calling me a lot."

"Tommy, Sarah is probably angry and needs time to cool off."

"No, Mom. This is serious. She's never done anything like this before."

"I realize that son." She paused. "Give it another day. If you still haven't heard from her, call me back and we'll track her down somehow."

"Okay mom. I'm just worried she won't want to marry me."

"Son, don't worry. I believe with all my heart that Sarah loves you."

Cindy knew that Sarah was just upset and needed some time away from Tommy. Women sometimes need time to cool off because if they don't, they'll *fly off the handle* and might do or say something that they'll regret later.

*   *   *

Peter and Sarah were having a great time. They went out to dinner; they laughed and danced the night away. They really felt more like friends than anything else. This was a night that Sarah never wanted to forget. She thought it was really nice having a gentleman to go out with during a time that her main man was trying to *burn the candle at both ends*.

The weekend came to an end. Peter dropped Sarah off at her car. She had parked it in an area where she knew Tommy didn't frequent. Sarah never told Peter that she was angry with Tommy. She never discussed him while she was with Peter. She believed that was something that was strictly between her and her man.

On the drive back, Peter told Sarah that she was really good company and asked if they could do it again sometimes. Peter also mentioned that he was sending her flowers. He didn't sign his name just in case she already had someone in her life.

Sarah said, "We sure can. I'm looking forward to our next getaway already." Peter smiled revealing his perfect teeth.

Sarah leaned over and kissed Peter on the cheek. "I enjoyed your company also. Call me."

Peter said, "You know I will."

Sarah jumped in her car and couldn't wait for Peter to pull off. She flipped open her phone, turned it on and found that Tommy had left her about a dozen messages. She had turned off her phone for the weekend. Instead of listening to Tommy's messages, she anxiously dialed his number.

"Where have you been?" Tommy spoke loudly into the phone.

"Oh hey, Tommy," Sarah said calmly.

The fact that Sarah was so nonchalant increased Tommy's anger. "Don't "oh hey" me," Tommy said. "You have no idea how angry I am, Sarah. In fact, I'm so angry that I'm tempted to call off the wedding. And if you pull another stunt like this again, I promise you, I will.

Sarah's stomach dropped a little when Tommy mentioned calling off the wedding, but she remained calm. "Hold up a minute, Tommy. Don't try to put this back on me. You know the reason why I left."

"Yeah because you were upset after checking my cell phone. Sarah, if you're looking for something, you usually find it. It's not a good idea to check other people's cell phones because you can misinterpret what you find."

"Misinterpret?" Sarah said, her voice louder than she'd intended. I didn't *misinterpret* anything. There's only one way to *interpret* numerous phone calls from the same woman." She paused for a few moments to regain her composure. "Tommy, I need a committed man in my life. Not a man who's going to play the field any chance he gets."

"Sarah, I admit I was wrong. But you were wrong to check my phone. I need a woman who will trust that I love her no matter what. I prayed and asked God to forgive me. Will you forgive me?"

Sarah almost started to cry and tell Tommy that she never wanted to see him again. Then she thought, I love this man, and I want to be his wife. She made Tommy wait a few moments before she responded. "I forgive you, Tommy. Just don't let it happen again."

Tommy said, "It won't, Sarah. But don't check my phone again. Can we have a relationship where we trust one another?"

"Yes," Sarah said. "That's what I want, also." She smiled. "I promise I won't check your phone again, if you don't worry and get upset when I go away sometimes."

Tommy said, "Look Sarah. The only way you'll be going away is with me or on business."

"Okay," Sarah said, still smiling, happy about the way the conversation had turned out.

Tommy said, "I'm on my way to your place to finish discussing our wedding."

"Alright, I'm on my way too."

They both arrived at the same time. Sarah looked like a new woman to Tommy. He wanted to question her about her whereabouts, but decided to move forward and only discuss their wedding plans. He ran over to her car, lifted her off her feet, hugging her tightly, covering her face with kisses. "You smell good," he said. "I missed you."

Sarah laughed. "I missed you too, baby. I couldn't stop thinking about you."

It was at that moment when Tommy knew that Sarah really loved him.

Sarah found that she had a lot of mail, including a letter from Tania confirming their next meeting with her a week from today.

Tommy left his phone in the car because he didn't want TerriLynn to call while he was with Sarah. He had already told her that they had to stop seeing each other. TerriLynn was heartbroken. She had once again fallen in love with another woman's man. TerriLynn was able to get Sarah's phone number from Tommy's cell phone one night when they were together. To make matters even more complicated, she had decided to give Sarah a call.

Sarah fixed sandwiches and chips for her and Tommy to snack on while discussing their wedding plans. He pulled out the brochures for Sarah to look at and they narrowed it down to two places, Hawaii or the Bahamas. Both places were beautiful and Tommy wanted Sarah to pick the place. She decided to go with Hawaii. She then asked Tommy if he would be ready next week to meet with Tania. Tommy assured her that he would be.

Tommy went home that night. He was still a little angry with Sarah, but at the same time, he wanted her more than he ever had. His desire for Sarah was so strong he thought it would be best if he went home that night. He was still determined to wait until their wedding night to consummate their relationship. Plus, he sensed that Sarah wanted to be alone. He could feel Sarah's vibe. He had tapped into her emotions just as a man should be able to detect his woman's feelings.

He kissed her and said, "I'll talk with you tomorrow."

"Okay," Sarah said. She was tired and couldn't wait to crawl into her nice warm bed. A few moments after Tommy left, Sarah's phone rang. She thought it was Tommy calling to tell her goodnight again. "Hello," she answered, with a smile in her voice.

"Hi, Sarah. This is #@&*^ calling to see if you are interested in a 3 day 2 night stay at a resort in the Bahamas. We are offering our customers a deal of a lifetime."

"Where are you calling from again?" Sarah asked.

"I'm calling from #@&*^ to offer you a place to getaway for you and a significant other to spend some time together on the sunny beaches of Bahamas. Does this sound like something you'd be interested in?"

Sarah said, "I am getting married soon, but I chose another place."

"May I change your mind and pick one of the places in this wonderful package?"

"No thanks," Sarah said, and hung up. She looked at her phone to see where the call came from, but it was a blocked number. Sarah thought that didn't sound right and every time the woman had mentioned the company's name, she couldn't understand what she was saying. She dismissed the thought and started preparing for bed. She had a very busy day tomorrow and wanted to get some rest. As she was getting in to bed, she thought, *there is no place like home even when the place you are staying is beautiful.*

The following morning, Sarah awakened with plans to call the wedding coordinator before going into work to confirm their appointment so that she and Tommy could meet with Tania.

After she showered and dried off, she put on her robe and picked up the phone. She already had Tania logged in so she pressed the bottom that said Tania.

Tania answered, "Hello, Tania White speaking."

"Hi Tania, this is Sarah calling to confirm our meeting and this time Tommy will be joining us."

"I will see you and Tommy Thursday at 7:00 p.m.?"

Sarah said, "That should work, but let me double check with Tommy and I'll call you later."

"Sounds good, thanks for calling. Bye," Tania said.

After hanging up with Tania, Sarah continued getting ready for work. She wanted to get into the office early to put some projects in order so that she could pass them on to someone.

While driving in, she called Tommy to check with him.

"Good morning," Tommy answered.

"Good morning, honey," Sarah said. "I was calling to see if we can meet with the Wedding Coordinator this Thursday at 7:00 p.m.?"

Tommy said, "Yes. I'll move some things around and be available. I'll pick you up from your place or the office. Just let me know where to pick you up Thursday afternoon."

"Okay, I'm almost inside the garage. I'll call you when I get settled in today."

When Sarah got into the office, she had flowers from Peter and this time he'd signed his name. Sarah laughed, because here her wedding day was getting closer and closer and Peter was still sending her flowers.

Sarah knew that she needed to tell Peter she was getting married; she didn't want to mislead him into thinking there could ever be anything between them. She decided to give him a call.

Peter's phone rang while he was in his office in the beauty salon. Peter said, "Hey, beautiful."

Sarah said, "Hi, Peter. Thanks for the flowers. How's your day going so far?"

"I'm enjoying my morning already and even more so now that you called."

"Thanks. Yes, I need to talk to you about something important. I was wondering if we could do lunch."

"Yes, I'm available around 1:30."

"Can we do lunch at 2:00? I have a meeting to attend and it might run over," Sarah said.

Peter said, "Sure. Anything for you, Sarah. Call me and I'll pick you up."

"Okay, I'll call you around 1:15 p.m."

Sarah rearranged her day so that she could meet with Peter. When it was time to call him, her phone rang and it was Tommy.

"Hello," Tommy said.

Sarah said, "Hey. I was just about to make a phone call."

"Were you getting ready to call me? Because I was calling to see if you wanted to do lunch today."

Sarah said, "Today?"

Tommy said, "Yes, Sarah. Today."

"I'll be in meetings all day today. Dinner would be better."

"Okay, we'll do dinner," Tommy said. "Leave your car at work and I'll pick you up for dinner and bring you into the office tomorrow morning."

"Sounds like a plan," Sarah said.

"Sarah, I really missed you when you were away this past weekend. I just want to spend time with you before we meet with the Wedding Planner. I'll talk with you later."

Sarah got up from her desk and removed the card from the flowers and placed them in the reception area. Her excuse was to let everyone enjoy them. She knew that if Tommy came to her office and saw the flowers, he would start to wonder. And she knew that Tommy could stop by at any time.

She called Peter to let him know that she wouldn't mind driving over to his shop to pick him up for lunch. Peter didn't have a problem with the change of plans.

Peter was waiting outside when Sarah arrived. He walked over and got into her car. "Hey gorgeous."

Sarah smiled. "Hi. And thank you."

As they were driving to a nearby restaurant, Sarah told Peter that in a couple of months she would be getting married.

Peter said, "Congratulations. I'm excited for you, but disappointed that I'm not the lucky fellow." He smiled.

"Peter, will you come to the wedding?"

"Sure," Peter said. "We can still be friends and conduct some business together. I'll always be here for you, Sarah."

Sarah felt a little sad and confused. Here she was about to be married and had met this wonderful man who was also marriage material. Not only was Peter a successful businessman, he knew how to treat women.

Sarah and Peter sat at a table in the back of the restaurant studying their menus. Sarah decided on the fried scallops, a baked potato with butter and sour cream and coleslaw. Peter decided on the salmon with spinach and mashed potatoes.

"Tell me about your plans for the wedding," Peter said as they waited for their orders to be taken.

Sarah said, "We're still putting on the final touches. We'll be meeting with the coordinator, Thursday evening." She really didn't want to go into details with Peter about her wedding so she changed the subject. She told Peter she wanted to make an appointment to come to his shop to get "the works."

Peter said, "Come by any time you want, Sarah."

This was really a dream come true for Sarah. She was getting everything she wanted from two different men. One, she loved and wanted to spend the rest of her life with, the other was turning out to be a really good friend. She decided that she wanted to remain friends with Peter.

The waiter took their orders and the food came out 10 minutes later. The service was great and the food was delicious. Sarah had to get back to the office and Peter was off for the rest of the afternoon.

He said, "Let's do it again soon."

Sarah said, "Yes, it was nice. Thanks for lunch."

When Sarah returned to the office, Tommy had called about 15 minutes earlier. She immediately called him to be sure that he was still picking her up. It was almost time to leave for the day.

"Hi, honey," she said when Tommy answered the phone.

"Hi sweetie, I'm not that far from your office. I'll be there soon."

"How soon?"

"In about 20 minutes. Meet me in front of the building. I'm really happy to finally have more time to talk with you about our plans."

Sarah said, "Fine. I'll see you then."

She ran to the bathroom to fix her makeup and comb her hair. Sarah went back to her office to shut everything down before she left.

On her way down on the elevator, she read an advertisement of Peter's salon. She thought, *and I just had lunch with him.*

Sarah ran to the car while Tommy had the door open. She kissed him on the lips and got in. Sarah was wearing White Diamonds by Elizabeth Taylor cologne and Tommy really liked how it smelled on her.

While pulling off, Tommy asked how her day was.

Sarah said, "It was an unusual day. I was able to get a lot done." Before going to lunch with Peter she was able to put together about 5 to 7 projects and pass them on to her staff. "How was your day?"

"I relaxed today because of this past weekend, I needed time to rest. I didn't get any rest when you were gone."

"Sorry, honey. I promise not to disappear again. And I'll be mature about handling any future misunderstandings we might have."

"Now, that's the Sarah I know and love," Tommy said.

Sarah was still full from eating lunch and really just wanted to go over the paperwork that Tania had given her. "Tommy, I'm not really hungry," Sarah said. Would you mind if we just went over the paperwork Tania gave me?"

"That's fine," Tommy said. "We can go over to your place and I can pick up a quick sandwich."

Sarah said, "Can we go to your place? This will be my first time."

"Sure we can go. I don't see why not."

"Cool." Sarah started rocking to the beat of the music that was playing.

Tommy liked Sarah's decision to discuss things rationally in the future. Every day Sarah said or did something that let Tommy know that she was the woman for him. "You know Sarah, you make me feel so comfortable and peaceful. After having a hard day, I can get with you and you just take away all my stress."

Sarah smiled. She felt the same way.

Tommy went through a drive-through and picked up a couple of sandwiches and some sodas. He thought Sarah might change her mind, so he got something for her just in case.

When they got to his place, Sarah started looking around. She noticed some photos that he had displayed and wanted to know who they were. "Who are these women?" Sarah asked, pointing at the photograph.

"My cousins," Tommy said. "They live in Philadelphia."

"Oh," Sarah said.

"Is there anything else you want to know?" Tommy asked, smiling.

Sarah smiled and shook her head no. "Let's just discuss these handouts."

"Whatever you say, honey." It wasn't that Tommy had never wanted Sarah to come over, it was just that he had his place set up more like a bachelor pad and he felt Sarah's place was more inviting.

Sarah was pleased and relieved that she found no evidence that any females had been in Tommy's apartment.

After they completed the paperwork and discussed the wedding, they went to Sarah's place. Tommy was spending the night so that he could take her to work in the morning.

Sarah took a shower and put on some comfortable clothes. She sat on the couch watching one of her favorite sitcoms while Tommy took his turn in the shower.

*   *   *

It was finally Thursday. When Tommy and Sarah walked into Tania's office, she was really happy to see Tommy. Sarah introduced them and they shook hands. At first Tommy didn't remember Tania until he and Sarah had sat down and he took a good look at her.

"Tania, Tania," Tommy exclaimed. "Don't I know you?"

"Yes, Tommy. We went to school together."

He laughed. He remembered that Tania would always be on his case about finishing school.

"Tommy, I noticed that you own your own business."

"Yes, I do. You won't charge me anything more because of it, will you."

Both Tania and Sarah laughed. They were really enjoying one another's company.

Tania said, "No, I won't. Let's get down to business."

Sarah handed Tania the paperwork that she and Tommy had completed. It was pretty clear about what type of service they were looking for.

Tania ended the meeting. "Let me look over what you have here. I'll contact you if I have any questions."

Tania loved doing business with people who knew what they wanted and who were easy to work with. Some clients, under the stress of planning a wedding, could be very difficult. Tania told them that she would meet them at the rehearsal at the church.

Tommy and Sarah left knowing that everything was set. Tania was on top of it. Sarah was delighted. Now she could focus on other things.

When they left the office, Tania started working on the invitations because Sarah had emailed her all of the addresses.

The ride home also went well. Tommy and Sarah didn't say a word to each other. They just rode home in a happy, comfortable silence.

THE BIG WEDDING DAY

When the 548 guests arrived, they stepped into a place in Singapore where the flowers were beautiful, with Palm trees everywhere, with backdrops of sandy beautiful beaches and tropical sunshine reflecting off the turquoise seas and different kinds of canoes hanging from the ceiling. Instead of getting married in Singapore, they brought Singapore to them. Their guests were in awe.

They were only expecting 300 guests, but a lot of people wanted to see Tommy and Sarah get married. Some came to support, while others came to see if it was really happening. Tania had already accounted for more guests.

Tommy and his Best man and Groomsmen were standing on the right side of the altar; Sarah's Maid-of-Honor and Bridesmaids were standing on the other side. As Sarah was walking toward Tommy on her father's arm, Surel, the gospel singer, sang "My Vow To You." Sarah had hired a professional gospel singer to surprise Tommy. The guests saw a tear drop from Tommy's right eye as he stared at his beautiful bride. It seemed as if she would never get to the altar. Tommy marveled at how lucky he was to have a woman like Sarah who would be spending the rest of her life with him. His heart felt swollen with love.

When Sarah and her father reached the altar, Jeffrey positioned her beside Tommy and looked at him as if to say, *I'm watching you.* He then said to Tommy before taking his seat, "Make her happy."

Tommy smiled and said, "Oh. I will."

Apostle Ellis waited until everyone was in position. He opened his Bible and turned to Tommy and quoted, "When a man hath taken a new wife, he shall not go out to war, neither shall he be charged with any business: [but] he shall be free at home one year, and shall cheer up his wife which he hath taken." (Emphasis added)

Before going on with the wedding vows, Apostle Ellis asked if there was anyone who had reason why this man and this woman should not get married. The place got really quiet. You could hear a pin drop. Tommy looked around the room to be sure TerriLynn was no where in the place. His heart started beating fast when a young woman stood up. But to Tommy's relief, she had to take a little girl to the bathroom. He wiped the sweat off of his forehead trying not to seem obvious.

Everyone turned to Apostle as he continued with the wedding ceremony.

Tommy's vows: "Sarah ever since I bumped into you when we were going into the grocery store, I felt a connection between us. I couldn't wait to run into you again. The thought of you would cross my mind even if I was with someone else. I didn't quite understand at the time, but I knew there was something about you that wouldn't leave my inner man. Because of you, I am the man that I am today. You complete me and make up the difference in every area of my life. You truly are the helpmate that I found. I love you, Sarah."

Sarah's vows: "Tommy, I love you, too, and I cannot see myself with anyone but you. When you are near me my spirit leaps for JOY. You take care of me mentally, physically, and spiritually. Your strength is greater than Sampson's who carried a gate out of a city. When you are not around, your scent is a sweet aroma all over me. I feel very secure when I'm with you. You protect me at all costs. When I bumped into you the second time, I knew that you were the man for me."

Sarah smiled as she continued looking into Tommy's eyes. He was mesmerized by how she looked and what she was saying.

Apostle Ellis had to get their attention as if they had drifted off into a sunset.

"Tommy, do you take Sarah to be your lawfully [wedded] wife and do you promise before God and these witnesses, to love her, comfort her, honor and keep her in sickness and in health, and forsaking all others keep thee only unto her so long as you both shall live?"

Tommy said, "I do."

"Sarah, do you take Tommy to be your lawfully [wedded] husband and do you promise before God and these witnesses, that you will love, honor and keep him in sickness and in health, and forsaking all others keep thee only unto him so long as you both shall live?"

Sarah says, "I do."

Apostle Ellis continues, "The ring." The Best Man went into his inside jacket pocket, pulled out the ring and handed it to Tommy. The guests could see the ring sparkling from a distance.

"Place the ring on Sarah's left hand, third finger and repeat after me. 'With this ring I place on your finger, which will signify how our relationship will be. It will never end.'"

Apostle continued saying, "Inasmuch as this man and this woman have in the presence of God and these witnesses consented together to be joined in the lawful bonds of matrimony and thereto have given and pledged their troth each to the other, I now, according to the ordinances of God and in the name of the State of Ohio, pronounce them husband and wife. What therefore God hath joined together let no man put asunder.

And now may the God of peace prosper and bless you in this new relation, and may the grace of Jesus Christ abound unto you now and always, Amen."[1]

When Apostle got to the end and said, "Now you may kiss your bride," Tommy grabbed Sarah and they kissed for at least five minutes. Some of the guests cried while some couples held each other close. You could feel love in the atmosphere. Karen heard a man whisper softly to his wife, "It will be your turn when we get home."

The photographer took more pictures. He was able to capture the look on some of the guests' faces when they walked into the room. He was also able to capture the ambience that was taking place when Tommy and Sarah kissed.

As they were leaving the building, some people threw rice while others blew bubbles. Sarah loved bubbles and felt that bubbles were very romantic. She knew what people said about rice causing birds to explode was a myth.

---

[1] The Pastor's Manual by J.R. Hobbs © 1962 Broadman Press Nashville, Tennessee.

She thought it was much better to blow bubbles because the rice on the church steps and on the ground could cause someone to slip and fall.

SCENES AT THE RECEPTION:

After the photographer took numerous photos of the family and the Bride and Groom, everyone jumped into their cars and headed to the reception.

When some guests had arrived, the band was already singing songs to get the celebration started. The music was nice and upbeat to keep the atmosphere charged. People started going over to the bar to get something to drink before dinner while waiting for everyone else to get there.

The Reception Hall was also set up as if they were in Singapore. Tania did it in both places. She hired only the best.

When the band noticed that the place had filled up fast, they started singing love songs for the bride and the groom as everyone was taking their seats waiting to be served. The waiters and waitresses were dressed as if they were from the island of Singapore.

Dishes that were served from the Singaporean foods which are a mixture of Chinese, Malay, Indonesian, Indian and Nonya cuisine with a sprinkling of Western flavour thrown in for good measure.[2] Dishes that were served are:

Indian Dishes - Vegetarian dishes; Roti Prata (Fried dough pancakes with a curry dip); Nasi Briyani (yellow pillau rice with nuts, raisins, spices) served

---

[2] www.royalplaza.com.

over chicken, fish or mutton. Mutton is a female or castrated male sheep.

Chinese Dishes - Chili Crab, Beef Hor Fun (Fried), Cantonese Roasts/Char Siew/Roast Pork, served over Duke Rice

Asian Cuisine - Thai

Western - All sorts of Seafood

Malay/Muslim - Fried Chicken; Malay Kueh; Otah (Grilled spicy fish paste wrapped in banana leaves)

Desserts - Malay Kueh (cakes and pastries), along with brownies, and different chocolates

You should have heard some of the conversations that were going on when the food was served. Someone said *at least they got fried chicken.* Sometimes new dishes can seem foreign. But when everyone started eating, all you heard was, *this is delicious.* And *let me try this and let me try that.* You also heard, *if you don't want this, give it to me.*

When everyone was almost done eating, the Best Man stood up and started clicking his glass with his spoon and everyone followed. Tommy and Sarah kissed for almost 60 seconds. The Best Man had to get their attention so that he could do a toast. Everyone laughed. The Best Man said, "You truly are a man to look up to, Tommy. I hope when I grow up that I will be just like you. Sarah, you have someone that will be with you, and Tommy, Sarah truly is the prize. I hope the best and continued success to the both of you. And, may God continue to hold you guys together forever. You deserve one another."

The band started performing again. The lights were dim and you could see revolving stars circulating on the walls. The mood was set for love. Tommy grabbed Sarah's hand and led her to the middle of the floor dancing to a slow jam.

Several minutes later an old friend of Sarah's tapped Tommy on the shoulder so that he could dance with Sarah. Women started running in a line behind Sarah so that they could dance with Tommy. When the guys noticed, they too started forming a line to dance with Sarah.

People were laughing and talking, while children were running around the dessert tables. Their family and friends were happy to celebrate with them.

Sarah's father, Jeffrey, stood by Ralph and said, "I'm finally letting my little girl go."

Ralph said, "I'm just glad that my son is marrying a virtuous woman."

Jeffrey looked at him confirming Ralph's approval of his daughter.

"I never thought that you were also checking to see if Sarah was the right fit for Tommy. Thanks," he said, as they were walking toward the Fountain of Youth. A name that Sarah suggested to make people think when they drank the coconut juice it was going to make them youthful as an eagle. The fountain flowed the entire evening.

It was time for the band to take a break, so they put on a slide CD. Instead of doing the Electric Slide, they did the Shuffle. This lasted for 20 minutes. Then it was time for the steppers to hit the dance floor. The next CD consisted of all the steppers jams. This was a celebration that they would never forget.

It was time for Tommy and Sarah to leave for their honeymoon. They had already packed and the limo picked them up to take them to the airport. After checking their luggage in on their way to board the plane Tommy saw TerriLynn walk past without looking at him. His heart skipped a beat. *What is she doing here?* he wondered. He shook his head and then looked again and said to himself, *she just resembles TerriLynn.* He sighed and felt at ease when he realized the woman was not TerriLynn.

When they were seated on the plane, Tommy didn't give a second thought to TerriLynn. Although Hawaii was many hours away, it seemed as if they had arrived in no time. Sarah was more excited than she'd ever been. She and Tommy held hands the entire flight.

Hawaii was more beautiful and romantic than Sarah could have ever imagined. The water was a shade of blue that Sarah didn't know existed. The weather was fantastic – around 77 degrees the entire time. They spent a lot of time soaking up the sun on the beautiful beaches, sipping tropical drinks; Sarah especially enjoyed the Blue Hawaii's and Lava Flows. She had wanted to try something different. But Tommy stuck to the Pina Coladas and Mai Tai's. They also went snorkeling, sunset horseback riding, on a volcano helicopter tour and a cave expedition. They even went parasailing, which Sarah thought was scary, but also fun and very exciting. She had squealed with delight as she and Tommy sailed 600 feet above the island. But despite the exquisite beauty of the island and the fun activities, Sarah enjoyed the time she and Tommy spent together in their luxurious hotel room the most.

When they got back home, Tommy and Sarah were still basking in the glow of the honey in the moon. Their honeymoon was one of those memories that could keep a couple together for a lifetime. They retrieved their luggage and went to the parking garage in the airport to get Tommy's car. He popped open the trunk to place their luggage inside. He immediately ran to the passenger side to open the car door for Sarah.

"Thanks honey," Sarah said.

Tommy couldn't wait to get home. They had decided to live in Sarah's condo until they found a house.

When they got home, they checked the mailbox and noticed that they already had received catalogs of homes in the area. Before they left, Sarah had notified different real estate agents that they were interested in buying.

At the entrance door, Tommy said, "Stop Sarah."

Sarah looked at him. "What?"

He picked her up and carried her over the threshold. She started kissing him all over his face saying, "I love you. I love you. I love you."

Tommy placed Sarah on the couch. "Later, I'll carry you into *our* bedroom," he said, smiling at his new bride.

After bringing in the luggage, Tommy sat on the coach and took off his shoes. He grabbed the remote as usual and found a basketball game playing. Sarah liked hearing men look at sports. She was trained well by her father.

*   *   *

Sarah's place was getting kind of tight. She only had one bedroom and one-and-a-half baths. They decided to take a day off and scheduled appointments to go see houses with their agent.

The first house they saw was too small. It reminded them of the condo. The second house they saw was beautiful, but Sarah didn't like how some of the rooms were laid out. They started getting tired and wanted to give up until another day when they came to a house with a drive up that looked like a small mansion.

Sarah gasped at the beauty of the house. "I love it," she said, before she'd even gotten out of the car.

Tommy said, "Let's go in and see if it's just as beautiful on the inside."

The agent unlocked the door. When Tommy and Sarah entered and saw the cathedral ceilings and large foyer with two pillars separating the foyer from the curved stairs that led to the upstairs rooms, both their mouths hung open as if it had been rehearsed. They walked toward the living room and noticed the beautiful bay window.

Sarah couldn't wait to see the kitchen. When they walked into the kitchen, Sarah almost fell over; Tommy had to catch her before she hit the floor. It was gorgeous. Stainless steel appliances, hardwood flooring, ceramic countertops, marble back splash, modern cabinets, and a sliding glass door leading to a deck. Sarah walked over to the doors and opened them. She stepped out onto the deck with Tommy following her. The backyard and landscape were something liked they'd never seen before.

Tommy said, "This must be an upscale area."

The agent shook his head. "No." These are middle class people who have good taste."

Tommy asked, "So what's a house like this going for?"

"Just $450,000," the agent replied.

Tommy and Sarah exchanged glances. "Just $450,000. Can you leave us alone for a minute please?" Sarah asked the agent.

"Take all the time you want," the agent said. "I'll be in the car if you have any questions."

Tommy and Sarah found another way to get to the upstairs. They hadn't seen the two full baths on the main floor. The hall outside of the upstairs bedrooms was really nice. The guest room had its own bathroom attached. The other two bedrooms had a shared bathroom.

When they walked down the hall to the master bedroom, Tommy exclaimed, "Oh my God!!!! Now this is a bedroom," as they got closer to the room. Sarah and Tommy were captured by the ceiling, which had a mural painted on it.

Tommy wondered who had thought to paint a masterpiece on the ceiling. Sarah was so overwhelmed with the beauty of it all, that she started to cry. They grabbed each others' hands and walked into the master bathroom; they relaxed in the whirlpool tub together while Sarah continued crying. There were two toilets with a wall separating them, two pedal sinks, two mirrors, two showers and one big whirlpool tub.

Sarah said, "Who would want to sell a house like this? I mean, who *wouldn't* want to stay in this house?"

"It doesn't matter," Tommy said. "We're sold. Let me get the agent to see what our next steps will be. I want to make you the happiest woman in the world, Sarah." Before he could run down the stairs the agent was already standing at the door with a wide smile on her face.

"What do you think of the house?"

"We'll take it," Tommy said, his smile wider than the agent's.

"Wonderful," the agent said. "I'm so glad that I could be of service to you and your lovely wife."

"Yes, we fell in love with the master bedroom."

"Have you seen the bathrooms down here on the main floor?"

"We don't need to," Tommy said. "We want this house."

"Let's go into the office because I don't believe you've seen the office or the basement."

When they walked into the office, which was already furnished, "Tommy said, "Oh my goodness. This office is already setup."

"Yes, this furniture was uniquely designed for this room so the previous owners didn't want to take it out; it comes with the house."

"Wow!"

Sarah had already made her way down to the main floor and had stopped to look at one of the bathrooms, which was a full bath. Then she went to the other bathroom and said out loud, "Another full bath. I'm going to have to get a housekeeper."

Tommy called for Sarah to come and see the office. When Sarah walked into the office, she looked from one wall to the other as she made a 360° turn.

Tommy said, "Sarah come sit at the desk so that we can go over what we need to do to get this house."

"Really, Tommy?' Sarah said tentatively. "You're going to buy this for us?"

"Yes, Sarah. I'm going to buy this house for you." You would think that the houses Tommy fixed up would be enough for them. But he wanted them to have a house that he hadn't worked on. They completed the deal and set a date to move in.

Tommy had a lot of money saved up, so they paid $225,000 upfront to be sure their mortgage payments would remain low; he was a smart man.

Sarah loved her new house. She had hired an interior decorator to help her furnish it and she loved every piece of furniture they'd chosen. The Italian leather sectional and matching chairs and chaise lounge; the art deco coffee table; the plush carpeting that she loved to sink her bare feet into; the bronze table lamps; the elaborate stereo system that Tommy had purchased and the 52-inch flat screen television. They had Romare Bearden prints and beautiful Mazzai Crystal masks on their living room walls that both their mothers prayed over. In the corner of the room was a half-moon shaped console table with pictures of family members, including pictures they'd taken on the honeymoon on it.

Sarah had especially enjoyed decorating the master bedroom. She had chosen a king size black ash canopy bed, matching dresser and chest of drawers. She had removed the carpeting and gone with a hardwood floor, which was always smooth and shiny.

Sarah and Tommy loved entertaining. Their family and friends were in awe of their lovely home. The parties were usually catered and when the weather was nice, they had them out on the patio. They always went out of their way to make sure everyone had a good time. Sarah often thought about how lucky she was to have a man like Tommy who had purchased her dream house. Sarah was happy; happier than she'd ever been in her life.

THREE YEARS LATER

Due to her hard work and dedication, Sarah had been promoted consistently on her job; she now managed three departments and her salary had increased dramatically. Tommy was proud of Sarah, but didn't like the fact that she spent so much time at work. He had cut down on his hours to spend more time with his wife, but Sarah refused to do the same. She worked late at least three to four times a week. And then on the weekends (if she wasn't working at home or didn't have to go into the office) she was too exhausted to do anything. Tommy started to feel that Sarah thought her job was more important than their marriage. They argued a lot and sometimes Sarah found that she'd rather be at work than at home arguing with Tommy. Why didn't he understand that her job was important to her? Why couldn't he be more supportive? Sometimes she thought that he might even be jealous of her success. Plus, the money she was making helped to support their lifestyle. *He should be happy*, Sarah thought.

But Tommy wasn't happy. He missed his wife. And he felt neglected. He couldn't even remember the last time they'd made love. Or for that matter, the last time they'd gone to a movie or to dinner or bowling. Sarah used to love to bowl. All they seemed to do when they were together was argue. Sarah had accused him of being selfish, but what was selfish about a man wanting to spend more time with the woman he loved? Once or twice it had even crossed his mind that maybe Sarah wasn't being truthful about working late. Maybe she had fallen out of love with him or was seeing someone else. He didn't want to believe that; and deep down he really didn't. Maybe he was just using that as an excuse to call TerriLynn, who he had been thinking about a lot lately. When he was with TerriLynn, she had made him feel like he was the most important thing in her life. He wanted to feel like that again.

One Friday night when Sarah was working late (she'd called him earlier and said she didn't know what time she would be home), Tommy was angry and bored and lonely. Without thinking, he dialed TerriLynn's number. After all this time, she sounded ecstatic to be hearing from him and that made Tommy feel good. He felt guilty about what he was doing, but the resentment he felt toward Sarah overrode his guilt. So, he invited TerriLynn out for a drink.

Sarah noticed that lately Tommy was never there no matter how late she got home. And when she was free on the weekends; he wasn't. He always claimed to have something to do concerning work. And several times when she called him on his cell phone, he didn't answer. When he did get in, which was always very late, Sarah refused to ask him where he'd been. She felt that he should volunteer that information to her, but he never did. Sarah was hurt and confused. Was her marriage over after only three years, she wondered?

One night, after working late and trying to flag down a cab to take her home, she saw Peter. He invited her out to dinner. They talked and laughed and enjoyed one another's company like she and Tommy hadn't done in ages. She knew it was wrong, but she told Peter that she wanted to see him again. And she did. She blamed Tommy for pushing her into the arms of another man.

Because of the way Tommy was treating Sarah, she had an affair with Peter. He went out the back door, while she went out the front door. Sarah was in a vulnerable place and Peter swept her off her feet. Whatever he said sounded like a spring of water flowing down from the mountaintop. It put her in a very peaceful state. She thought maybe she had made a mistake, that Peter was truly the one for her.

What Sarah did not know was that he was sent from the enemy to destroy her marriage. She was so happy. Peter kept her laughing. He was handsome and had a great sense of humor. She couldn't think of anyone but Peter. He took her on a tour of his business. She was so amazed. Sarah was able to get her hair done, manicure, pedicure, and massages once a week. She was already beautiful. Now, she looked as if she was stepping onto a Hollywood set. He would give her money to go shopping twice a week to the finest stores: Lord & Taylor, Macys, Abercombie & Fitch, and Ann Taylor.

Tommy was wondering what was going on with his wife. He knew something was different; however, he was caught up in a relationship with a younger woman who made him feel as if he was 18 years old again. TerriLynn was 23-years-old. One thing led to another and Tommy was even thinking about moving out. Then TerriLynn started harassing Sarah. She would call her at home, on her job, and even on her cell phone many times while Sarah was driving. TerriLynn didn't care about how many years Tommy and Sarah had been together. All she knew was that she wanted Tommy. And she was determined to get what she wanted.

*   *   *

One night, Rita called the girls over to discuss some things they had been going through. Jessica, Sarah and Carol arrived early, and they were still waiting on Sheila. The topic was how do you face your personal situations, stay focused, and move on to bigger and better things. You have to understand these four girls were strength to one another. They helped each other get to places of safety, prosperity and success.

Sheila finally arrived. Rita opened the door and that is when it all started. "Hey girls," Sheila said excitedly. They all pulled off of each other's energy.

Rita said, "Come on in. We were waiting on you. You're the piece of our puzzle that completes us."

Sarah exclaimed, "You know that's right."

These girls knew that the networking they did between one another not only kept them financially stable, but it helped them take notes from one another: from hair to clothes; from shoes to purses. Their style was so unique that they became trend starters.

Carol asked, "Who wants something to drink?" All at once Rita, Sheila, and Sarah said, "I do."

Carol said, "Hold up. I'm not asking you guys to marry me. You say 'I do' to your man when he proposes."

They all laughed, except Sarah.

"So, Sarah how's married life treating you?" Rita asked.

Sarah opened her mouth to answer and started crying a well full of tears. "Tommy's so busy these days with what I don't know. He's changed."

All the girls rushed over to Sarah.

"I'm sorry, Sarah," Carol said sadly. She rushed into the kitchen to get the drinks believing that it would make Sarah feel better. But once Sarah started drinking, her feelings came pouring out. The girls had to put their meeting to the side and comfort her. They didn't want to give her too much advice about how to handle it because they wanted her to make her own decisions.

Sheila said, "No matter what Sarah, hold on to your man. Don't let anything separate you from him."

"I know that's right," Carol said. "I'm waiting on a man right now to come into my life and can't seem to find the right man."

Rita said, "You see that's our problem. We're trying to *find* a man when we're supposed to just be *ready* when *he* finds us."

"You know what I mean," Carol said. "Every date I go on the guy is either *too* something or *not* enough something. I can't seem to connect with the right guy."

Sheila said, "We better get back to Sarah. She needs us more than we think. It's not easy being married to a fine man like Tommy. Heck, he's got it going on."

Sarah was crying even harder. Rita grabbed a box of Kleenex® and kept handing Sarah one at a time to wipe her tears. Carol retrieved a garbage pale to dump the napkins in. When the pale overflowed, Sheila would run and dump it. Jessica was there for moral support.

These close friends really supported one another. Once Sarah started feeling better, they danced and laughed to try and keep Sarah happy. Then they decided to call it a night.

*　　*　　*

Tommy changed his mind about leaving. He loved Sarah and wanted it to work out between them. They had a lot going on and had signed important contracts together binding them financially. They decided to go to the church several blocks from where they lived. Instead of driving, they made up their minds to walk after conversing for about two hours on what they should do. The conversation went from what we should wear, to do we own any Bibles. They both agreed to walk. They were a bit nervous because they hadn't been to church in a while; neither of them had time to attend church services.

They admired the beautiful scenery during their walk. The manicured lawns with dynamic floral patterns took their breath away. There was one moment that they stopped walking and stared at the blue, red, pink and purple Hydrangeas. The flowers were so beautiful that Sarah said she wanted to hire someone to take care of their lawn. Tommy tried convincing her that he was totally capable of taking care of their yard.

What brought them back to earth were three small children, speeding along on their bikes. Tommy grabbed Sarah to move her out of their way. She stumbled, almost falling into the grass. Tommy said, "whoa, Nellie."

"I'm okay," Sarah assured him. "Let's get to church before the service is over."

They walked into the front door of the church and were blown away by the beautiful edifices. The architectural design was out of the ordinary. There were cathedral ceilings and stain glass windows. The front was setup like going from the outer court, through the holy place, pass the veil that had been torn in two, to the Holy of holies.

Apostle Ellis, who married them, was the Pastor of The Tabernacle of the Kingdom in Ohio. Apostle operates in the Apostolic and Prophetic anointing. Tabernacle was a place where the Shekinah glory dwelt. It was a place of healing and deliverance. The anointing of God was full in that place. The ancient ruins were restored. When you walked in the door, the yolk that had you bound, fell off you and the intercessors knew how to destroy every yoke of bondage as they prayed prophetically. The anointing in this place caused demons to cry out and say, "It is not our time. Why torment us?"

Apostle has a very strong men's ministry that taught men how to be kings and priests. He showed them the dynamics of operating spiritually, physically, and naturally. Apostle Ellis is Prophetess Wanda's husband. Wanda gave Apostle Ellis a prophetic word that came to pass. He admired her and couldn't wait to run across her path again so that he could develop a relationship with her. Apostle Ellis believed in having a relationship with people as well as with God. He's proven that a relationship with God is important because it helps when dealing with people.

Apostle Ellis had organized programs set in place that taught and then activated their skills, gifts, and talents. The men at his church outnumbered the women. Apostle had a strong ministry and when women found out about this ministry, they told their female relatives and friends, so Apostle had in place a women's ministry that Prophetess Wanda was over.

They were almost to their seats when Apostle Ellis asked that the visiting friends and family please stand. He asked that they remain standing until one of the ushers gave them a booklet about the church and a card to fill out so that they could receive a free gift at the end of service in the bookstore. Tommy and Sarah stopped and stood still. This was all new to them. Tommy was thinking about one of the dreams he had in New York when he had to go up a lengthy flight of stairs to get to the church that was up on a hill.

This church was quite different from many churches. Before Apostle Ellis got up to minister the Word of God, the prophets took turns prophesying to the congregation and confirming and judging one another's prophesies. These four women were called the "Daughters of Philip." (Acts 21:9) It was amazing. Tommy and Sarah had never heard anything so uplifting before. They had missed the Praise and Worship part of the service.

The Word of the Lord that went forth spoke about their present and future. The prophets explained to the congregation how the things that happened to them in the past was only a journey they had to travel to get them to the next realm, the next dimension. The word of knowledge of the past and the word of wisdom of their present and future was in effect. The Spirit of the Lord was flowing in that place of safety. When you come together with the men and women of God, it should be a place of protection.

It is so important that we understand what the prophets are saying and that we take what they say to the Lord before acting on anything that has been prophesied. The Word of the Lord that went forth did three things (comfort, edify, and exhort). Tommy and Sarah just sat and listened.

After the prophets, the intercessors got up and prayed one after another over the congregation. One of the intercessors sent forth a prayer in the Heavenly for Prophetess Wanda's birthday:

**A prayer for my spiritual mother, First Lady,
Prophetess Wanda of The Tabernacle of the Kingdom
HAPPY B-DAY:**

"Father God in the name of Jesus, I thank you for giving Prophetess Wanda another birthday this year. Lord, renew her youth as an eagle and give her long life upon this earth. Father thank you for the truth that is in her inward parts and the wisdom that is in her hidden parts.

Lord, take Prophetess Wanda to higher heights and deeper depths in you. Stir up her strength, power, courage, and the gift of God that you already placed inside of her. She has shown and proved over the years that walking with You will transform lives because Your Word says if You be lifted up from the earth, You will draw all men unto You. She is a worshipper who loves and adores you. Her life exemplifies it.

Prophetess Wanda is a woman of honor, a woman that is very well respected, a woman that is full of wisdom, a woman that walks in integrity; whose intuition is always on point, a woman who nurtures and trains her natural and spiritual children, who not only teach us what to do but show us by walking in Your percepts. You made her a royal priesthood, a holy nation, a peculiar woman. She is a kingdom woman.

Lord, cover and protect her from all hurt, harm and danger. Place warring and ministering angels around Prophetess Wanda to protect her and give her a Rhema word from the Logos that will sustain her. When she is hurting, pull her into Your bed chambers where you can rock her in Jacob's bosom. Unfold Your glory and minister to her inner woman where it would manifest everywhere she goes and in everything she does. Develop a deeper intimacy with her to give her more revelatory knowledge of Your Word.

Bless her financially, at net breaking point, where she would have an overflow to be able to meet more than her needs and her heart's desires. Give her more vision to establish businesses and place those around her that will follow the vision as she writes it and makes it plain.

Lord, you knew that she not only needed spiritual intimacy but natural intimacy as well, so I thank You for Apostle Ellis who you gave her to. You brought Eve to Adam just like You brought Prophetess Wanda to Apostle Ellis. The man of God has been trained to sanctify and cleanse her with the washing of water by the Word. Cause a deeper relationship between her and Apostle Ellis where their love for one another will always be fresh and renewed. Let them never get complacent with what to do when they are in the presence of one another. I thank you for the long lasting love you placed in them to show couples it is better to marry than to burn.

Lord God, I thank You that she is able to identify the giftings and skills that You have given us to operate in. She is so connected to You, that she is also able to discern when it is time for us to move forward. I thank you for the relationship she has with You to help train and build up the body of Christ.

I thank You for the natural womb and spiritual womb that incubates her natural and spiritual children to nurture, train, and raise us to full maturation. Jesus, I thank you and praise you for her.

May the words of my mouth and the meditation of my heart be acceptable in your sight. It is in Jesus' name I pray, Amen (And It Is So!!!)"

Tommy and Sarah thought WOW!!! What an amazing church service. They started wondering if this was too much for them, but it felt so right. Isn't it something while the things of God are going forth, the enemy tries to get in and deter God's people to think negatively?

The intercessors prayed earnestly. They covered all bases of one's life. There were some that prophetically prayed, while others prayed the scriptures. Before you knew it the entire church had come from the Outer Court and passed the Holy Place and had now entered into the Holy of Holies past the showbread, candle sticks, bowls of incense, curtain torn into two pieces; into the place where the mercy seat was where the Ark of the Covenant now resides. The Spirit of the Lord had exposed some hidden agendas, where some partners started crying out and moaning as if Jesus Christ was standing right there in front of them.

The musicians had received the Spirit of the Lord upon them where they played under the anointing. Tommy and Sarah felt like falling to the floor under the unction of the Holy Spirit. Before they knew it, they grabbed one another's hands and fell to their knees. Sarah got really emotional, while Tommy tried keeping his composure. This was their first time attending, and he didn't want to go too far. His pride had gotten in the way until suddenly, he saw an angel appear in the room where it seemed as if it was only him and the angel.

The angel began to speak to Tommy. *"Tommy, Tommy, Tommy. You have been given a mantle when you were in New York to unlock people out of their distress. Stop fighting with God and surrender so that you can be used by the Lord, Jesus Christ. Remember it is only through the blood of Jesus that God's grace is sufficient. You cannot keep running and hiding under a rock. Step out in FAITH and believe that God had already prepared you to do mighty exploits in the earth. Know that God got your back and your front, your going in and coming out. He knew you before he placed you in your mother's womb. Tommy, God will never leave you nor will He forsake you."*

Tommy started perspiring as if he were standing under the showerhead with beads of water splashing on him. He was experiencing a washing and cleansing by the Holy Spirit. Sarah noticed that there was something going on with Tommy and she started calling his name, "Tommy, Tommy, Tommy." Sarah didn't know the rule not to bother someone as long as the Spirit of the Lord was dealing with them.

Once receiving Jesus Christ to be your personal savior, you must journey on a path of learning and being taught how to operate correctly and in order. He thought it was the angel trying to get his attention, again. He wiped his forehead only to find out that others in the congregation had gone into a whole new realm also and some were still caught up. There was no going back. This day would change Tommy and Sarah's lives forever.

Once everyone had made it into the Holy of Holies, Apostle Ellis got up and told the congregation to say good morning and Happy Birthday to his lovely wife, Prophetess Wanda. He told them that she was their spiritual mother, and that she was coming forth to read the church announcements. He mentioned that he wanted to get the church to a place where they would listen and understand that the church announcements were important. After Prophetess Wanda read the announcements, the choir sang the song, "Give and it shall be given to you, press down, shaken together and running over," while the tithes and offerings were being served unto the Lord.

This took Tommy and Sarah even higher into the Spirit realm. They were thinking how much can the flesh take. But again, it felt so right.

Apostle Ellis had the praise team sing a prophetic song of the Lord before he delivered the message. As soon as the Praise Team finished singing, Apostle Ellis went straight into his message.

THEME: BE A MASTER BUILDER AND BUILD UPON A SOLID FOUNDATION

It is my prayer that as you are listening to this message, that you will receive a great assignment to create more.

To build is either to bring about something that has not existed in the natural realm or to repair something that has already existed and was broken down or ruined. God wants to use our hands in the Spirit and in the natural to bring about what has existed before and the new things (to us) that God wants in the earth, or to repair the breach that was broken.

Before the foundation is laid, we have to dig a big hole. In the Spirit, we will dig a hole when we pray and seek the Lord concerning the foundational structure and what to actually build. The more you pray, the larger and deeper the hole gets. Our time spent in prayer determines how deep and wide our foundation can be which ultimately determines how tall we can build.

Also, we must count up the cost because when you build, it will estimate at one cost, but while you are building you will find it is going to cost more to complete the project. Add an additional amount of money to the estimated cost. This will show that you are a wise builder.

If you have a set time to finish the project, allow for more time because time can get away from you while you are building.

Let's deal with the foundation first:

Please turn your Bibles to: I Kings 5:17 and it reads, "And the king commanded, and they brought <u>great stones</u>, <u>costly stones</u>, [and] <u>hewed stones</u>, to lay the foundation of the house."

We must be sure that the foundation is solid as a rock. Because once we lay the foundation and build thereon, sometimes the foundation will start cracking when it settles. Keep in mind, the crack (disobedience) should be fixed in order that it doesn't keep cracking. A cracked foundation can cause seepage (sin) to come in and cause water damage.

Matthew 7:24-27 reads, "Therefore whosoever heareth these sayings of mine, and doeth them, I will liken him unto a wise man, which built his house upon a rock: And the rain descended, and the floods came, and the winds blew, and beat upon that house; and it fell not: for it was founded upon a rock. And every one that heareth these sayings of mine, and doeth them not, shall be likened unto a foolish man, which built his house upon the sand: And the rain descended, and the floods came, and the winds blew, and beat upon that house; and it fell: and great was the fall of it."

Obedience is better than sacrifice. When we are obedient, we will eat the good of the land according to Isaiah 1:19. Now, when the storm comes and the winds blow, our house will stand because we built it upon a solid foundation.

All while we are building, for most, we are focused on what we want to accomplish. But some will get off course, especially when it seems as if it is going to take forever to complete the project and we cannot see the finished work.

We must train ourselves to take this natural body pass what it is used to. When you are working on something and you start thinking you cannot do anything more, keep going. Don't stop. You will find that you can do more than your body limits you to do. When you see an obstacle in your way, move it out of your way and keep going. This is easier said than done. But speak those things that be not as thou they were. (Emphasis Added – Romans 4:17)

When I'm getting ready to do something, I always tell people, "Guess what I'm getting ready to do." And then I start telling them exactly what I'm getting ready to do. My whole conversation is about what I'm getting ready to do. I wake up to it, eat it, drink it, and sleep it until it is complete, and I move on to the next thing. There will be some who do not care about what you are getting ready to do. It doesn't matter. Even those who you think care, might not.

The writer in I Kings 5:17 talked about three types of stones to use to lay the foundation. And, they are: <u>great stones</u>, <u>costly stones</u>, and <u>hewed stones</u>.

GREAT STONES - Great - Hebrew word gadowl (ga-dole') which is an adjective meaning large; in number; in intensity loud; God Himself; great, distinguished (of men), important things.[3]

Since great stones is listed first, I will explain what I hear the Spirit of the Lord saying about the word 'great.' We must first seek the Kingdom of Heaven and His righteousness and all earthly things shall be added. This is building with God Himself. He will instruct us on how to build and what to build. This way we will exuberate greatness and become great, distinguished (of men). And, even receive a large amount to work with, which is very important when we build.

Stones come in different sizes: large or small and contain different minerals and metals. Some stones come from substance underneath the ground, while some are in the mountains. Stones are also created when volcanoes rupture and explode lava which cools off and a rock is formed. They are all common in a natural state. Think of a stone as strength, firmness, and something solid. King David used a rock, which is common to slay Goliath.

We want to be sure that as we are laying the foundation that our hearts do not turn into a stony heart. Anything we build, we want it to come from the Heart of God. While praying, we must ask specifically what God wants in the earth. Because whatever He desires in His heart will become a desire in our heart when we ask. Then we can delight ourselves in the Lord and He will give us the desires of our heart, which will be His heart's desires.

God already sees us as Spiritual Geologists who study the things of God. We studied the Old Testament (OT) and see what God did back then. We even studied the

---

[3] www.blueletterbible.org

New Testament (NT) and are able to read what God did during that time. This is the history and the process of how God works. Now, we are watching carefully that God is doing a new thing. It shall spring forth. The springing forth is the actual material that is used of the manifestation of what God is doing. We can still follow God's pattern from the OT and the NT to determine if it is God or not. And, when our prayers cause an explosion in the realm of the Spirit, we become Spiritual Volcanologists. It is what comes after the explosion that proves the results of the totality of what God is doing in our lives and what will happen when we depend on Him.

COSTLY STONES - Costly - Hebrew word yaqar (ya-kar') it is an adjective meaning valuable, prized, weighty, precious, rare, splendid, highly valued, jewels, glorious, splendid, weighty, [and] influential.[3]

When we lay the foundation using costly stones, we want to be sure that we use the best and only the best. We want the stone that is heavy, rare and highly valuable, to be the precious jewels that we use for material. We want to use the Stone (JESUS) that the builders rejected—the Chief Cornerstone. Stones can be precious Gems.

HEWED STONES - Hewn - Hebrew word gasiyth (ga-zeth') feminine noun a cutting, hewing.[3]

To actually take a stone and hit it until it is chopped into smaller pieces will take time and effort to accomplish what we are set out to do. So, be patient and enduring. Like a flint. Be steadfast and unmovable. Because to get what you really want to accomplish, you must develop patience and patience is a virtue. FAITH already sees the vision done. James 1:34 says, "Knowing [this], that the trying of your faith worketh patience. But let patience have [her] perfect work, that ye may be perfect and entire, wanting nothing."

While you are building, do not complain. Focus only on the task in front of you. Follow the guidance and leading of Holy Spirit who gets His instructions from our God, our Lord.

When an architect builds, he/she first sees it in a vision and then writes an algorithm listing every step needed to take to bring the vision into existence. Once the algorithm is written, a flow chart can be created which helps the builder know that Plan A is to flow this way; however, along the way God can change Plan A. If so, the flow should go another way. Plan B can also show an addition to the building once Plan A is complete. After the flow chart, you go into designing a floor plan that consists of all the rooms, doors swinging interior or exterior, windows opening, main fixtures (kitchen, bathroom, and laundry room items - permanent fixtures, etc.).

Whatever you are building, remember Plan A is what God has already implemented. When changing Plan A, be sure that it is God and not you. Because God can take what we have and alter it in whatever way He sees fit. Allow Him.

As I close, remember these stones:

The tablets (stones) that God wrote the Ten Commandments on that Moses carried back to the people.

The stone that was rolled back and Mary of Magdalene could not find Jesus and the angel of the Lord said, He has risen.

Isaiah prophesies in Isaiah 32:2 about Jesus being protection in a windy place, a hidden place from the storms, a river of water in a dry place, and something solid in a place where you can become tired and exhausted about life itself. And the scripture reads,

"And a man shall be as a hiding place from the wind, and a covert from the tempest; as rivers of water in a dry place, as the shadow of a great rock in a weary land."

Bottom line is, Jesus is the Rock in a weary land.

Simon was also referred to as a stone:

John 1:42 says, "And he brought him to Jesus. And when Jesus beheld him, he said, Thou art Simon the son of Jona: thou shalt be called Cephas, which is by interpretation, A stone."

"And I say also unto thee, That thou art Peter [PUT YOUR NAME HERE], and upon this rock I will build my church; and the gates of hell shall not prevail against it." (Matthew 16:18)

We are considered lively stones: I Peter 2:5 says, "Ye also, as lively stones, are built up a spiritual house, an holy priesthood, to offer up spiritual sacrifices, acceptable to God by Jesus Christ."

During Biblical times, Altars were built out of stones to signify endurance, immutability, and solidarity.

I thank God that I'm standing on a Solid Rock (JESUS)—the Chief Cornerstone. A foundation that cannot be shaken. Won't you stand with me.

Harvest Time
The congregation stood to their feet while the praise team sang a prophetic song:
You're my Rock in a weary land,
You're my Strong Tower,
I will, continue, to stand upon You,
You,
You,
and only You,
You're my Rock in a weary land.
You are my Rock.

Apostle Ellis asked the congregation, who among them was ready to give their lives to Christ. He told them that they could come under Christian experience or with a letter from another ministry giving them the right to come, or as new babes in Christ. Potential partners began running down the aisles to the front of the church while the ministers stood in front holding out their hands bidding them to come. As the new partners came forth, ministers would greet them in the aisles. Intercessors were on their knees at the altar praying for the Spirit of the Lord to unction the people to come.

Apostle asked if anyone needed prayer and that intercessors would come and pray for them. This service was full of the GLORY (Kabod, Hebrew word – Shekinah, Greek word) of God. You could feel the crispness of the fresh air blowing with a sweet scent in the air.

While Tommy and Sarah were sitting on the main level, there were sparkles of gold coming down from the ceiling. They both blinked to get a clear view of what was happening. It was unbelievable.

Tommy began to see an open vision of him entering into a house through the front door. What he noticed is as he walked toward the back of the house there were stairs and these stairs led to the basement. When he got downstairs in the basement, he noticed that there was a man standing in front of him, while a lady in a red dress was standing along side of him. The lady never moved from her position, but the man extended His hand toward Tommy. He looked around and noticed on one side there was a room that was dark and gloomy, while on the other side there was a fish tank built in the wall. There were large fish of many different kinds in the tank with lots of beautiful colorful plants. Tommy started thinking how the fish were surviving, and the man spoke, *I know you are wondering about the fish tank. The previous owners had a built-in system that would feed the fish and a filter that would clean the tank so that the fish would survive and live forever and never lack.*

Tommy looked ahead and saw rooms in the back of the basement that really needed cleaning out. *Tommy, I came to assist you in dealing with these different rooms. These rooms are in representation of what is going on inside of you. The room that looks dark and gloomy is how your spirit man feels when you keep dealing with the woman in the red dress. The rooms in the back that need cleaning out, is the sin that so easily beset you that must be removed from you because every time you try to get ahead, these rooms keep calling you back into them. The fish tank is in reference to how God will supply your every need according to His riches in glory which is by Christ Jesus. God will continue dealing with you to assist you in every endeavor of your life. Trust Him, He wants you to have everlasting life!*

Tommy came out of it and thought WOW!!! He looked toward the front of the sanctuary and noticed that a lot of partners joined that day.

It was amazing. Tommy grabbed Sarah's hand and they both ran down to join the ministry together.

After taking in the new partners, there were administrators in line to take the new partners over to another room so that they could feel out forms and receive a prophetic word from the Lord through the assign prophets.

Apostle gave the benediction. He said all rise, while holding up his right hand. He said, "Now, unto Him who is able to keep us from falling and to present us faultless before His presence with exceeding joy; to the only wise God our Savior, who gave us dominion and authority both now and forever, let us all say, Amen. May the Lord be with us as we travel from this place. (Emphasis Added)

As Tommy and Sarah were walking home, they did not speak a word to one another. They joined church that day. Finally, Tommy spoke. "Let's talk over dinner. Right now I'm trying to take in what just happened."

"Me, too," Sarah said, still enthralled by what she had experienced.

*   *   *

Weeks had gone by and Tommy and Sarah had gotten involved with the church and started taking classes that led them to operate in their giftings. They were also interested in learning more. Both Tommy and Sarah brought something to the table because they were both educated with Master degrees.

The drugs in the community and gang violence had gotten out of hand. The Bloods and Crips were infiltrating Ohio with drugs and gun trafficking. In the community they convinced young people to join them, to work for them to take over territory, and engage in violent crimes.

Apostle Ellis and his partners evangelized in these areas to convince young people not to serve the Kingdom of Darkness. Apostle came from the street so he pretty much knew what to expect. He trained the evangelists how to approach these unlawful characters so that the Kingdom of Heaven (Light) would advance.

Prophetess Wanda was also trained in the art of taking people to their next level and building women to be women that walked in their dominion and authority. She taught the partners of the church to walk in the power that God had already placed in them. She would identify their giftings and train them to operate properly. She would give them examples of the women in the Bible. The midwives, the difference between the Hebrew women and the Egyptian women, women of wisdom, Midian women, women of Jabeshgilead, concubine women, singing women, lewd women, foolish women, outlandish women, harlots, strange women, honourable women, silly women, aged women, young women, holy women, pitiful women who ate their children, mourning and cunning women that prayed for nations, and the list goes on. Prophetess Wanda would describe each kind of woman and then ask the women how do they identify with these different women.

The church is setup for the whole body. This information was typed on the hand-out Tommy and Sarah received as new partners.

There are classes in:

Economics

Office Procedures

Computer Analysis

Computer Engineer

Construction

Carpentry

Landscaping

Sexuality

Anatomy of the body

Nursing

Personal Hygiene

Prayer/Fasting

Hearing from God

Prophetic Prayer

Intercessory Prayer

Teachers' Training

Training to Preach with Notes and w/o Notes

Unveiling the Scripture

Type and Shadow

Strong's Concordance Teachings

Stirring up the Gifts of Holy Spirit,

The Gifts that Jesus left when He ascended (5-fold ministry – Apostle, Prophet, Teacher, Evangelist, and Pastor)

The Gifts from the Father

The Educational System (Grammar School, High School, Trade School, College-degrees)

Music (Gospel, Hip Hop, R&B, Rap, Jazz, Classical, Country Western, Pop, Latino, Raga tone, Reggae, Rock, etc.)

Family

What is a Husband?

What is a Wife?

Being a child in Education, Chores, and Ministry

Being a teenager

Teenage Pregnancy

Being a Young Adult

Bachelor

Bachelorette

Parenting

Government Structure

Legislative Laws

Jurisdictions

Business classes (C Corporation, S Corporation, LLC, Sole Proprietor)

Accounting

Finance

Interest Rates

Credit Scores

Real-estate

There was also a state of the art gymnasium in the church, workout instructors and personal trainers to keep the partners fit.

This ministry was known across the globe to teach and activate you spiritually, mentally, and physically. Apostle Ellis would show his partners of the congregation that the Lord meant for them to operate in a full body dimension. This way you will be a balanced saint not so heavenly bound you are no earthly good. He showed them when God designed us; He took us out of His thoughts, His vision, His very being and brought us forth. His vision of us unfolded.

We were there and heard the conversation that took place that said, "let us make man in our image after our likeness." Because of this Apostle Ellis was able to take the partners of the congregation and show them that everything they desire and everything they want is locked up inside of us in a place called potential. He taught his partners how to visualize it in their minds and then write it down and from there, speak it into existence, and then act on it. His famous words were taken from a passage of scripture that says, "faith without works is dead." He stirred his partners up with the most HOLY FAITH. He would build them and encourage them that God designed us with a purpose in mind.

Apostle Ellis also took the partners of the church tithes and offerings and put them in an interest bearing account and at the end of the year during Christmas time; he would bless his partners pertaining to how much interest he gained on their tithes and offerings. This was a wonderful system. Because of this, the partners gave more money throughout the year while investing less in their 401Ks, and they knew they couldn't depend on their pension plans or Social Security. During tax season, they were able to write-off what they gave to the church as a tax shelter.

Prophetess Wanda conducted a class that asked a question to her students, "Have you received the Holy Ghost since you believed?" She told her students you must first believe before you can receive the Holy Spirit. Do not receive Him by way of your intellect, but let His Spirit connect with your spirit.

Prophetess Wanda asked her students, by the showing of hands, who wanted to receive Holy Spirit. She explained that when Jesus Christ died on the cross and was put in a tomb, He rose on the third day. When Jesus ascended, Holy Spirit descended upon the earth. According to the scriptures, Holy Spirit dwells in our belly where living rivers of water flow. Once you receive Him - receiving means you will allow Him to operate in your life. He is in there, but you have to activate the Spirit of the Lord through praise and have a lifestyle of worship.

You allow the Spirit of the Lord to use you so that God will get the glory. Prophetess Wanda led her class to the book of I Corinthians where it lists the gifts from the Holy Spirit. It also shows, if you are operating in the gifts without LOVE, you sound like sounding brass and tinkling cymbals. She also added that you can operate in the gifts with sin in your life because they come without repentance. She told them but sin would hinder you from operating in the fullness of the gifts. You will operate in them; however, you will have on your mind the sin that you committed. She added, "Should we remain in sin?" as Paul asked and answered, "God forbid."

Prophetess Wanda taught what each gift is and how to operate in them. She trained her class on activating in the gifts every day. It was time to lay hands on those who wanted to receive the Holy Ghost. Prophetess Wanda asked, "Who wants to receive Holy Spirit?" About ten students raised their hands. She told them to get in line. The first person who stepped up was trembling. Prophetess noticed and started singing a song of the Lord. She explained that, that will take them out of the mindset of the natural and usher them into the Spirit. This went on for at least half an hour. Her intercessors were praying in tongue while she was ministering to the saints while singing a song of the Lord.

The first person that had stepped up was now receptive to receive the endowment of the Holy Spirit. Prophetess had a couple of her intercessors stand on both sides of the person and two more stand right behind her. She told the member to raise her hands to the Lord and when Prophetess laid hands on her, the member immediately began to speak in tongues of fire. The partners who were watching began to cry out to the Lord and they too wanted to receive Holy Spirit. This went on for hours. People who were not receptive changed their minds. After two hours, they prayed a closing prayer and those who received Holy Spirit went to their destinations excited about what had happened.

* * *

In the church of Apostle Ellis and Prophetess Wanda, each room has a name. The prayer room is called the "Intercessors Nest" - it is a place where travailing takes place. One area is where God pregnant you with vision. Another room is where the travailing actually takes place, and the other is where the birthing comes forth.

In a totally different room the teaching of nurturing, then the teaching of taking the vision to the next level - next dimension; and raising the vision to full maturity.

This is why Apostle's church is growing and maturing; men came from everywhere to be endowed with vision, carry it full term and not aborting it or miscarrying it, to bring it through the birthing canal with travail and then bringing it forth. Apostle allowed Prophetess Wanda to teach the women as well as men how to be mid-wives. Because iron sharpens iron, the visions and dreams came forth, nurtured, and brought to full maturity through the help of others. It seemed as if they were real doctors and nurses working in a maternity ward. Everything had to be clean and sanitized. Prophetess Wanda would always have everyone wear white in this room. This room was also all white. It had a big flat screen TV on the wall that only played preaching and gospel tracks. There were rooms attached to the main room that were altars of different anointings. There is also an area called Solomon's porch.

There was a questionnaire that everyone had to fill-out. Prophetess would seek the Lord concerning each one. She knew that she needed the Lord to guide her and direct her to the visions of her partners, while Apostle taught the partners to follow the vision of the church.

You would think that it would be a conflict of interest but what they found was, the visions and dreams were common. They were all for the up building of the Kingdom.

The men, women and children did not walk in fear. They walked in the admonition of the Lord. Apostle ministered the Word of God, so the partners had strong FAITH in what God could do. He wasn't focusing on members that left to visit other ministries. He knew in this time and in this season, partners could come and they could go. Apostle Ellis focused more on the assignments that God gave him which was always fresh and new.

Prophetess, in all her classes, would always sing a song of the Lord that said:

I only trust you, Lord,

I don't even

trust myself

I don't put my trust in man

because man has failed me every time

I only trust you, you Lord.

This song would ring through the bellies of the partners until they realized that their trust should be in God. This took the pressure off that they had to do everything by themselves.

The partners were so mature that they stopped walking independently but interdependently. It was so awesome to see the partners work together while operating in their individual giftings. They allowed the Holy Ghost to freely maneuver through them. To see them in operation made other churches that would come to visit, catch on "fire."

About 125 partners immediately were interested; they ran over to the Gilgal room so that they would be able to get a seat. This room seated about 100 people. After they sat down and those left without a seat stood around, Jessica stepped in front of the room and explained to them why there was a yearning in their spirits to be there. She was really gifted, and it showed in the books she had written.

Jessica said, "Class, if you are truly interested in giving up all the illicit activities in your life, the Lord can truly use you for the building of His Kingdom and for the edifying of the Body of Christ.

She asked them, "Are you ready?"

The class answered with a resounding, "Yes!"

Jessica said, "Well, let me explain exactly what the Birthing process is all about.

"First, the Lord will pregnant you with a dream/vision, and then you have to carry it for a length of time. Some might carry it for a short period while others might carry it a lot longer. There could be a number of reasons why one would carry a dream/vision for a certain length of time. During the term of the pregnancy, you will experience cravings of certain foods and a pulling of an urgency to study certain scriptures of the Bible.

"Secondly, we will teach you how to eat certain foods and study the Word of God to give your dream/vision the nutrients needed to develop it properly while you are carrying it.

"Thirdly, we will take you into the birthing room when it is time where the midwives (man deal with men and woman will deal with women), would assist you in bringing forth the dream/vision. In this room you will lay prostrate on the floor, praying, mourning, crying, sweating, and doing whatever it is going to take, to birth your dream/vision.

"Fourthly, once the baby is born, you go into the recovery room (some don't have to go into this room). It depends on if we have to watch you closely before taking you to either the UIC or to the room of maturation. Do not pay attention to others and the process they will go through. Focus only on yourself because this is your baby that you will be birthing.

"Once the dream/vision is fully grown, there is another process you will go through to be sure that the dream/vision continues to grow, expand and multiply. Some will even pass their babies at a certain time to someone else to continue the life of it.

"In each and every one of these rooms prayer is always in order to continue what you have to go through in the development for you and your dream/vision. Does anyone have any questions?"

A member in the class spoke. "I'm a little nervous about this and am not sure if I am in the right position to go through with this. Will there be one on one sessions so that I can talk to someone?"

Jessica said, "Sure. After filling out the forms that are on the desk, we will evaluate them and then meet one on one to talk with you and see if you have anymore questions about the steps you are going to take. Also, throughout the time of the development, we will make time to meet with those who need one on one attention.

"We are going to experience something we can pass on to others that are interested in the birthing of dreams and visions. Keep in mind, just because you will complete this course does not mean that you are ready to deal with the downside of this. Yes, there is a downside.

"The downside is when you have not been trained properly, you might take a person through the process and forget something. Always do it with a team of people so that there will be judges who will see things you might miss. Never deal with this alone. It is critical that you are hearing and listening to what I am really saying.

"Throughout this development and after your dream/vision is fully developed, remain humble because if you are not humble, the opposite of it is pride. And pride comes before a fall. Are there any more questions?"

Another potential participant raised his hand and asked, "Will there be any handouts or material based on this class?"

Jessica said, "Yes. When you look through the information in front of you, you will find the particular books we are looking for you to purchase in the church bookstore. Take the information home, fill it out, look it over, and if you have any questions, email me or wait to see me next Sunday after service in this same room. You can just drop off your filled out information package, and keep the curriculum for your reference.

Closing prayer is to bind the spirit of Shebna and release the spirit of Eliakim. Shebna had personal motives and agenda. Eliakim was concern about doing what the Lord said for His people.

"If there are no more questions or comments, I will see you next Sunday after service."

Everyone left with the anticipation of birthing their dreams/visions.

Sarah asked Tommy, "Do you feel something in your belly jumping around?"

Tommy said, "I sure do. Not only do I feel something moving inside my belly, I also feel a tingling throughout my hands and my feet."

Sarah started laughing. "Let's go and get something to eat so that we can discuss what just happened."

Tommy said, "That sounds good because I'm truly hungry. Isn't it something when we receive from the Lord, it depletes all the food we ate? It seems as if we have been healed and when we eat natural food afterwards, it replenishes the nutrients our body needs to function. Also, have you noticed that once we get home, we take a nap so that we can rest our bodies?"

Sarah said, "Yes. I thought I was the only one who noticed that."

They got in the car and drove off. There was a great restaurant near the ministry that served home cooked meals. When Tommy and Sarah walked inside, they saw Jessica, so they waved. Tommy asked for a table for two, but there was a ten-minute wait. While they were waiting, more people entered the restaurant. The area was getting kind of tight. Sarah went to the ladies room while Tommy waited to hear his name called.

When Sarah came out of the ladies room, the waitress sat them in a booth where they could be pretty much alone. The food was delicious. After they ate, they immediately left to go home and rest.

Although, their marriage was better, Sarah didn't spend as much time at work anymore and they attended church on a regular basis, Tommy was still seeing TerriLynn. He wasn't seeing her as much as he used to anymore, which TerriLynn definitely didn't like, but Tommy still felt the need and desire to be with her. He knew he had to break it off and he prayed that he would be released from whatever hold TerriLynn had over him. But so far, he felt his prayers hadn't been answered. He knew that the flesh was weak and that he had to pray more fervently.

One night, after they'd gone out to dinner, Tommy was driving TerriLynn home. While on their way, he looked in the rearview mirror and thought someone was trailing them. Every turn they made, this car made. They didn't know what to think. When Tommy turned down the block where TerriLynn lives, the car trailing them kept going straight. Tommy was relieved; he thought that the guilt he felt about cheating on his wife had him imagining things.

Tommy pulled up fast and TerriLynn got out of the car. She was walking up the path to the front door of her building when suddenly a cat ran over her feet. She jumped back and screamed.

Tommy rolled down his car window and asked, "Is everything alright?"

TerriLynn laughed nervously. "It was a cat that came out of nowhere. I'm okay. I'll call you before you make it home to let you know I made it upstairs."

Tommy said, "Okay. sweet dreams."

Since Tommy was near his parents' house, he decided to stop by for a visit. The car that was following them made him wonder if his wife knew about his affair with TerriLynn. He knew that Sarah was aware that TerriLynn was calling him in the past, but Sarah had made good on her promise and never checked Tommy's cell phone again.

Tommy pulled up in front of his parents' house. Although he had a key, he rang the doorbell because it was kind of late and they weren't expecting him. Cindy got up from her chair and went to the door wondering who it could be.

Tommy knew she was staring through the peephole. "It's me mom. Tommy."

Cindy opened the door. "Tommy, what are you doing out this time of night?"

"I was in the neighborhood and thought I'd stop by and see how you and dad were doing," Tommy explained.

Cindy thought it was strange for Tommy to be "in the neighborhood" at this time of night when he lived across town.

"Where's dad?" Tommy asked.

"He's downstairs working on something," Cindy stated.

"I won't bother him," Tommy said. "Let me get something to drink before I head home."

Cindy said, "I made some fresh lemonade just like you like it."

Tommy went to the bathroom and washed his hands. He stared at himself in the mirror. *What am I doing?* he silently asked his reflection. *Why can't I let TerriLynn go?"* He proceeded to the kitchen, grabbed a cup out of the cupboard and rinsed it. He walked over to the refrigerator, removed the pitcher and started pouring the lemonade into his cup. He was pouring so fast that some spilled and splashed on his shoes. "Oh man!" he said.

"What's wrong, Tommy?" Cindy asked.

"I spilled lemonade on my Gators," Tommy said angrily.

Cindy handed him some wet wipes. After Tommy cleaned his shoes, he headed home.

Tommy turned on WENZ 107.9 FM R&B station because it was about an hour and fifteen minute drive. As he was on the road, Sarah called. Tommy answered. "I'm on my way home. It should take me about an hour and fifteen minutes."

Sarah said, "Okay, I'll see you when you get in."

"You don't have to wait up. I'll let you know when I get there."

"Okay drive safely."

*   *   *

One of TerriLynn's neighbors left the main door to the lobby cracked and someone came in, quickly and skillfully picked her lock and entered her apartment. TerriLynn thought she heard something. She sat up in bed, stared at her bedroom door, and listened intently. She listened for a while, almost holding her breath, but heard nothing. She decided it had been her imagination and a few moments later was fast asleep.

The person that came in stood still because he'd heard TerriLynn moving in bed. Several minutes later, the intruder entered her bedroom, tiptoed over to her bed, and placed a cloth saturated with chloroform over her nose. She struggled in her sleep for a moment, before she was rendered unconscious. He then took a needle from his pocket, tapped on the side of it, and stuck it in her arm. It was full of pure heroin. He picked up TerriLynn's limp body and wrapped it in a sheet. He grabbed the keys to her car, walked quickly down the stairs, ran to her car, and drove it to the back of the building. He went up the back way to get her. Glanced around to make sure no one was looking, placed her in the trunk of her car, and made the long drive to Lake Erie Coastal Ohio. He knew that TerriLynn was dead and the thought of it made him happy. He had already driven his car to the area and took a cab near TerriLynn's place.

After reaching his destination, he sat in the car for several moments to be sure the coast was clear. He removed TerriLynn's body from the trunk, placed her in the driver's seat, and pushed the car into the lake.

Three days later, some fishermen discovered a car that had floated to the top of the lake and immediately called the Columbus, Ohio Police Department because it looked as if someone was in the driver's seat.

The Police, fire department, emergency tow truck and ambulance came on the scene. Once they all got there, the Police roped off the area with yellow and red tape and questioned the guys who found the car. Once the emergency tow truck got the car out of the water, they discovered a woman in the driver's seat. At first, the Police didn't know if this was someone who committed suicide or someone had committed murder. The body had been in the lake for three days and was badly decomposed. The coroner would have to determine the cause of death.

The news reporters arrived on the scene. One of the first on the scene to report the accident was a popular newswoman named Jeanna Dee. "Good morning. This is Jeanna Dee from NBS News reporting that a car was found in the lake by three men who were fishing. Once the vehicle was pulled out of the water, Police made a frightening discovery: a body of an African-American woman clad in her pajamas was behind the wheel of the car. There was no identification on the victim and the cause of death is unknown. There will be more on this story once the details come in. This is Jeanna Dee, NBS News."

Once the body was identified as TerriLynn, the Police started their investigation. They went to her place of residence, found her cell phone, checked the numbers on the phone, found out the identities of the callers, and started bringing them in for questioning. When they found

Tommy's phone number in TerriLynn's cell phone numerous times, they decided to bring him in first for questioning.

Sarah was shocked and confused when the Police showed up at her door asking for Tommy. They asked him to step outside so they could speak to him alone. After a few moments, Tommy came back in looking distraught. He told Sarah that a friend of his had been killed and the Police wanted him to come down to the station to ask him some questions.

"Who?" Sarah asked, shocked by Tommy's revelation. "And why do they want to question you?" Her eyes were wide with fear.

"We'll talk about it when I get back," Tommy said.

"I'm going with you," Sarah said.

"No," Tommy said, his voice rising. "We'll talk when I get back."

Sarah wasn't used to Tommy raising his voice. She stared at him with a worried expression.

Tommy touched her cheek and spoke gently. "Everything's going to be fine, Sarah. I'll tell you everything when I get back. Okay?"

Sarah nodded. Then Tommy pulled her to him and hugged her.

When Tommy got to the Police station, he sat in a small room with a mirror (which he knew was a two-way) waiting for the detectives to come and question him. He felt terrible about what had happened to TerriLynn. He didn't love her, but he'd never wished her any harm. He also felt terrible about continuing his affair with her. He knew that Sarah would be devastated when she found out. He only hoped that she would be able to forgive him.

The autopsy had been done on TerriLynn's body. The cause of death was ruled a homicide. They found the chloroform in her system and since there were no other track marks on her body, it was determined that someone else had given her the fatal dose of heroin. They had checked her apartment and found that her door had been tampered with. They had also taken fingerprints.

The Police informed Tommy that he wasn't a suspect, but that he was a person of interest in TerriLynn's death. They told him that he had the right to have an attorney present, but Tommy waived that right. He had done nothing wrong. All he had to do was tell the truth.

Tommy told the detectives how he'd met TerriLynn. How long he had known her. And how long he'd been having an affair with her. The detectives questioned Tommy about the other men in TerriLynn's life, but Tommy could offer no information about any other men TerriLynn might have been seeing. He had often gotten the impression that he was the only one. She made herself available any time he wanted to see her. He was suddenly flooded with shame about the way he had used her.

They asked him if his wife knew about his affair with TerriLynn and Tommy told them that she had in the past, but she thought it was over. He told them that he had dropped TerriLynn off that night and then went to his parents' house. They told him they would check with his parents to confirm his alibi. They told him they were going to bring his wife in for questioning.

"My wife had nothing to do with TerriLynn's death," Tommy said loudly.

"You don't know that, sir," one of the detectives said. "Maybe your wife *did* know about the affair. Maybe she was having you followed."

Tommy was incredibly angry that they could think that Sarah could be capable of murder. "I told you, my wife didn't even know I was still seeing her. I told her it was over and she believed me."

"Maybe she *didn't* believe you," the other detective said.

"Maybe she thought you were lying," the first detective said.

"And, after all, you were lying," the second detective added, with a smirk.

Yes, Tommy thought. I was lying. And I've been unfaithful to the woman I love. And possibly ruined our marriage and both of our lives. And all because I allowed lust to take over my heart and my mind. Tommy lowered his head in shame.

"Or maybe TerriLynn was going to tell your wife," the first detective said, leaning over the table, his face very close to Tommy's. Tommy knew he was trying to intimidate him, trying to make him lose his cool. Although Tommy was nervous, he remained calm. All he needed to do was continue to be truthful.

"TerriLynn wasn't going to tell my wife. She knew I wasn't going to leave Sarah for her," Tommy said.

"Maybe *she* told your wife and your wife didn't tell you," the detective who had been in his face said. "Maybe your wife decided to take matters into her own hands."

"That didn't happen," Tommy said, angrily. Not for a single moment did he believe any of the things the detectives were implying about Sarah.

The detectives exchanged glances, then stared at Tommy for a long moment. Tommy stared back at them.

Thanks for coming in, Mr. Whitfield, the first detective said, with a fake smile. "You aren't planning on leaving town anytime soon, are you?"

"No, Tommy, said, "I'm not."

"Good," the second detective said, "because I'm sure we'll be needing to talk to you again. And we *will* be bringing Mrs. Whitfield in for questioning."

Tommy took a taxi home wondering how he was going to break this to Sarah. He told the driver to take the long way so that he could think. When he finally arrived home, Tommy opened the front door with disgrace on his face. He walked over to Sarah who was sitting on the sofa nervously wringing her hands, sat down next to her, and told her everything.

Sarah sat next to Tommy on the sofa crying. She was inconsolable and it was breaking his heart. He tried to put his arm around her, but she moved away.

"You've been lying to me all this time," Sarah said.

Tommy didn't say anything.

"Why?" Sarah asked.

Tommy still didn't respond; he didn't know what to say.

"Did you love her?"

"No, Tommy," said. "I love you, Sarah. I always have."

"Then why, Tommy? Why did you continue seeing her?" All this time, Sarah had been feeling guilty about the fact that she'd been seeing Peter. But she had broken it off with him when she and Tommy had started attending church. Peter had called her a few times at work after that, but she refused to see him. And eventually, he had accepted her decision and stopped calling.

Sarah wanted her marriage to work. She had been tempted to tell Tommy about Peter, but was waiting until what she thought was the right time. Her guilt had kept her awake at night. And all this time Tommy had been seeing TerriLynn.

Sarah was sorry that the woman had been murdered. But Tommy's affair had caused them both to be suspects in her murder. Tommy had told her that the Police would be calling her for questioning. She was hurt, angry, confused, humiliated and terrified.

"I ... I don't know why, Sarah," Tommy said. And that was the truth. "You and I weren't getting along. It seemed as if you would rather be at work than at home with me. And TerriLynn was there. She was always there whenever I wanted to see her. She *wanted* to be with me when it seemed like you didn't. But I never loved her, baby. "You've got to believe that."

Sarah glared at him. "How can you expect me to believe anything you say to me ever again, Tommy?"

"It's the truth," Tommy said. He reached for Sarah, but again, she moved away. He knew that at that moment, she hated him. And she had every right to. But he also knew that the love was still there, under all the pain and hurt and fear like a buried treasure. And if he had to dig the rest of his life, he would find that treasure again. "We'll get through this, Sarah," Tommy said gently.

Sarah bolted from the sofa. She was crying again. "Will we, Tommy?" she yelled. "Will we?" She ran sobbing from the room.

The following day the Police asked Sarah to come in for questioning. Like Tommy, she decided against having an attorney present. She had nothing to hide. They questioned her for about an hour and a half while Tommy waited for her in the waiting room. They asked her about her marriage and about Tommy's affair with TerriLynn. They asked her whereabouts on the night that TerriLynn was murdered. Sarah answered all their questions truthfully. Then, like they had told Tommy, they told her not to leave town and said that they might need to question her again.

Tommy and Sarah rode home in silence, each in their own deep, sad, frightened thoughts.

The Police tried to find others that might have had a reason to murder TerriLynn. They talked to her friends and neighbors. The Police also tried to contact her relatives. Her parents were dead, but they were able to locate her foster parents who told them that when TerriLynn turned 17, she had left home one night with her 19-year-old boyfriend, Eric Sony, and then called them that night to tell them that she wasn't coming back. They never saw her again. They had guided TerriLynn from the age of 12 and said that she had always been a wild, difficult child. And although they were saddened, they were not surprised that their foster child had come to a bad end.

A couple of weeks later, the Police caught two breaks in the case. A woman who lived in TerriLynn's building came forward and gave them a description of a man she'd seen hanging around the building a few times late at night. Then a woman who had been picked up for prostitution, who wanted to stay out of jail, told them that she had some information that might help them with a murder case.

The woman's name was Mimi. She had been working the streets with TerriLynn years ago. They both worked for a pimp named Eric Sony. Eric was brutal and sadistic and after working the streets for a year, TerriLynn ran away. Eric had promised that he would find TerriLynn and kill her for leaving him.

A week after TerriLynn ran away, Eric went to prison for attempted murder (he beat one of the women who was working for him almost to death). Mimi said that Eric was released from prison a few months ago and she'd seen him in a bar. He told her that he had found out where TerriLynn lived and that he planned on making good on his promise to kill her.

Mimi had thought Eric was just talking crazy because he'd been drinking quite a bit, until she heard on the news that TerriLynn had been killed. The description Mimi gave the detectives fit the description of the man who had been seen hanging around outside of TerriLynn's building.

Mimi told them the name of the bar where Eric hung out and the Police went there and staked it out. When Eric showed up, they arrested him. After interrogating him for hours, Eric finally broke down and confessed, saying that he did say he was going to kill her, but hadn't. But he showed no remorse about TerriLynn's murder. Although he told them that she met with a certain trick every Tuesday evening for the entire night and this trick paid big money for her.

The Police found the man exactly in the place where Eric said he would be. They took him down for questioning, while other cops went to his apartment. They found several items that caused Marc to be the suspect in the murder of TerriLynn.

Although Sarah was relieved when she heard that they'd found TerriLynn's killer, she still didn't know whether she wanted to stay with Tommy. She didn't think she could trust him again. And, although she still loved him, she didn't know if she would be able to forgive him.

Tommy remembered the emotional trauma he put women through before he got married. He had done the same thing with Sarah, but he was determined not to lose her. He made sure that he catered to her every need. He comforted her in every way possible. Perhaps he hadn't been ready for a commitment. Maybe that's why he had strayed from their marriage. But, after almost losing Sarah, as well as his freedom, (and almost causing Sarah to lose hers), he realized that the way to have a happy, healthy marriage was to commit totally to his wife and to God.

Tommy wanted to start over. He knew he still had her love, but he had to rebuild her trust. And he knew that would take some time. He would not attempt to make love to Sarah until he knew that he had her forgiveness.

They went out on dates – to the movies, plays, bowling, dancing, roller skating and to dinner at Sarah's favorite restaurants. They lay in bed and talked for hours. They learned little details about each other that they hadn't previously known. They attended church every Sunday. They received marriage counseling from their Pastor. Tommy told Sarah that he loved her everyday. He held her and let her cry; she still cried sometimes. Sarah cut down on the hours she worked so that she and Tommy could spend more time together. They were almost like newlyweds again except for the lack of lovemaking.

One night, Tommy ordered crisp curried shrimp for dinner, keredok and sago pudding for dessert - some of the dishes they'd had at their wedding reception. The meal had been delicious and it reminded Sarah of their wedding day. The promises they had made to each other in front of God, their relatives and their friends. Memories of that day brought tears to her eyes. After dinner, they cuddled on the sofa and watched a movie.

After the movie, Sarah told Tommy about Peter and asked for his forgiveness. He was hurt, but he knew that if he wanted forgiveness for his own transgression, he had to be willing to give it in return. That night, after he kissed Sarah goodnight, they lay silent for a few moments, and then Sarah reached for her husband.

Tommy took the experience he learned in the past and showered Sarah with LOVE. Tommy learned to really love himself and that is how he was able to come away from a life of infidelity. A man that loves himself, will give up his life to love his wife just like Jesus gave himself for the church. Tommy knew that the bible says, a man that finds a wife, finds a GOOD THING and obtains favor from the Lord. He wanted his favor as he told his father before he got married.

THE BEGINNING

Sarah asked Tommy if he could take her to this bed and breakfast restaurant on Saturday mid-morning so that they could discuss the possibility of selling their home and moving to a house built from the ground up. Sarah always wanted to do this and she was hoping that Tommy would go along with it, but she didn't want to pressure him.

Author's Bio:

Kathy McClure is President, CEO and CFO of McClure Publishing, Inc. Since she's been in business, she has become one of the most influential Publishers in business. Kathy writes in all genres, so she decided to publish many different genres to keep her audience interested. Her main goal is to stir-up the readers' creativity so that their imagination can go as far as they could imagine. If they can imagine it, it can come true. Her purpose is to transition others to bigger and higher places.

Kathy is a motivational speaker and teacher who motivates her listeners to go far and beyond their expectations of life. She combines natural things with spiritual things to bring about the power that we possess in walking in our God given authority. She is a worshipper, an intercessor, who operates in the prophetic and apostolic anointing. On the business level, she is an administrator in her family life, business and secretary of one of the biggest law firms around the world. She also finds time to cook and serve those in homeless shelters and loves to teach and activate them on how they can live their lives to the fullest and not settle for less. Kathy is committed to doing radio shows of many different teachings and interviews of those interested in exposing their talent, gifting and skills to the public.

In order to contact the author, please write to:
McClure Publishing, Inc.
9624 S. Cicero Avenue
Oak Lawn, IL 60453
Or call: 800.659.4908
Email: mcclurepublishing@msn.com

A Man Praying for His Wife

by: Kathy McClure

McClure Publishing, Inc.
www.mcclurepublishing.com
800.659.4908

A MAN PRAYING FOR HIS WIFE

I.   I WILL LOVE HER AS THE WEAKER VESSEL

> *(I Peter 3:7a)* "Likewise, ye husbands, dwell with them according to knowledge, giving honour unto the wife, as unto the weaker vessel . . .,"

A.   The Relationship in the Garden Jehovah Shammah (the Lord is there), You put me to sleep and You opened me up and from the seat of my affection, you created woman. The void that took place after the spiritual surgery has always been by my side. Every time I become intimate with my lovely wife, that void gets fulfilled. I will chase her in my home as if we were in the Garden of Eden playing and running around the trees. As I breathe the freshness of her cleaning, it will be as the fresh air you provided in the garden. When I embrace her, it will be as if I am holding something I never want to let go. When I look upon her, I will be captured by her beauty from within. I will look deep inside of her to see areas that need prayer. I will pray a prayer that will mend every pain and hurt from her past. I will try and understand what she goes through each and every day of our lives. Your Word says, in all your getting, get an understanding.

Genesis 2:2 *"And the LORD God caused a deep sleep to fall upon Adam and he slept: and he took one of his ribs, and closed up the flesh instead thereof;"*

Genesis 3:20 *"And Adam called his wife's name Eve; because she was the mother of all living."*

Proverbs 4:7 *"Wisdom is the principal thing; therefore get wisdom: and with all thy getting get understanding."*

B.   God Designed Her for Me

Elohim (God, Judge Creator), You saw that I was lonely, so You decided to create for me a helpmeet. When I first looked at who you created for me, I said, "WOW MAN" (woman). Being her architect you made sure that she came with all the special parts and the lovely curves for my hands to embrace. I thank You for the woman You put in my path. Teach me how to be patient with her and show her exactly what you created her to do. Let me not take advantage of the authority You gave me over her. Cause her to trust me even when negative thoughts run across her mind. Let her see me as her knight in shining armor. I want to please her in every way. Give me insight on what her needs are, that I may meet them before she even asks.

Genesis 2:18 *"And the LORD God said, It is not good that the man should be alone; I will make him an help meet for him."*

Genesis 2:20 *"And Adam gave names to all cattle, and to the fowl of the air, and to every beast of the field; but for Adam there was not found an help meet for him.*

Genesis 2:23 *"And Adam said, This is now bone of my bones, and flesh of my flesh: she shall be called Woman, because she was taken out of Man."*

C.   Strengthen Her to Endure the Pains of Life

King of kings, whenever my wife is weak, strengthen her. For You said in Your Word that when we are weak then we are made strong. For Your strength becomes perfected in our weakness. Build her up wherever she might be torn down. In the empty dark places inside of her, fill them with Your Glory. Pull her out of the state of depression and oppression that will try to suppress her.

Release her from the hand of the enemy. Cause her to walk in fear. Destroy every demonic force that makes her feel defeated. Restore her from the inside where it will manifest in how she walks and talks. Give her strength to know that she has power to cast mountains into the sea. Give her confidence to know that she shall have whatsoever she says.

II Corinthians 12:9 *"And he said unto me, My grace is sufficient for thee: for my strength is made perfect in weakness. . . ."*

Matthews 21:21 *"Jesus answered and said unto them, Verily I say unto you, If ye have faith, and doubt not, ye shall not only do this which is done to the fig tree, but also if ye shall say unto this mountain, Be thou removed, and be thou cast into the sea; it shall be done."*

D. Cover Her Tomorrow

Alpha and Omega (the Beginning and the End; the First and the Last), You cared for her before she came into existence when she was just a thought in your mind. Fulfill my wife's day that she will not wonder about tomorrow. You said that You would take care of the sparrows everyday and You cause the lilies not to spin when the wind blows. I could just imagine how much You want to meet all of our needs. Your Word says, not to worry about what we are going to drink or eat and neither what clothes we are going to wear. Lord equip me with more than enough so that I will provide for my wife's needs that she doesn't have to worry about anything. I want her to live comfortably in our home where she can be the virtuous woman You ordained her to be. Let her hands build up our home and not tear it down. Teach her how to express herself in a loving way where I can hear every word that she speaks because she will win me over by her conversation. Let her not wait until tomorrow to tell me something is bothering her, but let her express it today before the sun goes down. Encamp warring angels around her to go with her from day to day. God go before her and make every crooked way straight. Give her favor with man. Make provision for her before she gets to the places You originally ordained her to be in.

Proverbs 12:4 *"A virtuous woman is a crown to her husband: but she that maketh ashamed is as rottenness in his bones."*

Matthew 6:26 *"Behold the fowls of the air: for they sow not, neither do they reap, nor gather into barns; yet your heavenly Father feedeth them. Are ye not much better than they?"*

Matthew 6:31 *"Therefore take no thought, saying, What shall we eat? or, What shall we drink? or, Wherewithal shall we be clothed?"*

Matthew 6:34 *"Take therefore no thought for the morrow: for the morrow shall take thought for the things of itself. Sufficient unto the day is the evil thereof."*

Isaiah 45:2 *"I will go before thee, and make the crooked places straight: . . ."*

I Peter 3:1 *"Likewise, ye wives, [be] in subjection to your own husbands; that, if any obey not the word, they also may without the word be won by the conversation of the wives;"*

E. Cover Her Mind

Oh my Heavenly Father (Abba Father), regulate her every thought. Stand at the gate of her mind that every thought will submit to the obedience of Christ. Pull down every stronghold that would try to exalt itself against the knowledge of Jesus Christ and bring into captivity every thought to the obedience of Christ. Prosper her that she would be in health even as her soul prospers. Every lie that the enemy is tormenting her with, destroy it right now. Cause Your Word to be in her thoughts where Your Word will counterattack the works of the enemy. Keep her mind stayed on You that she will be in perfect peace; give her peace that surpasses all understanding. Cover her eyes and ears (entrance gates) so that evil will not enter her thought pattern. Let the blood of Jesus flow in her mind and cancel the assignment of blood clots forming. Cause her mind to retain information and recall information. Let me not do anything that would cause her to lose her mind. Let her thoughts be good toward You and me. Keep her sane and regulate her thought pattern.

II Corinthians 10:4 "*(For the weapons of our warfare are not carnal, but mighty through God to the pulling down of strong holds;)*"

II Corinthians 10:5 "*Casting down imaginations, and every high thing that exalteth itself against the knowledge of God, and bringing into captivity every thought to the obedience of Christ;*"

Isaiah 55:10 "*For as the rain cometh down, and the snow from heaven, and returneth not thither, but watereth the earth, and maketh it bring forth and bud, that it may give seed to the sower, and bread to the eater:*"

Isaiah 55:11 "*So shall my word be that goeth forth out of my mouth: it shall not return unto me void, but it shall accomplish that which I please, and it shall prosper in the thing whereto I sent it.*"

F.   Cover Her From Head To Toe

Jehovah Nissi (Banner of Protection), Let Your blood run down from her head to her toes. Place a shield of protection around her everywhere she goes. I speak healing to every inch of her body. Cause her heart to pump blood where oxygen would be released to clean her blood flowing through every vein. Clear her lungs so that she will not have a respiratory problem. Go into her stomach, kidneys, liver, and intestines (upper and lower) to cause them to function the way You designed them. Keep her female organs covered with Your blood that cancer will not set in to kill her. Strengthen her legs to get her around everywhere she needs to go. Lord, teach her to soak her feet and take care of her body. If there are any medical problems she has with her body, give her wisdom to pray for healing before going to see a doctor. And if there is any area of her body that I forgot to touch, touch it right now.

Remove any disease and affliction that have set up camp inside her body to destroy her. Cause her to feel good about herself. Remove any doubt she might have concerning her body structure. Build her self-esteem where she will complement others and speak affirmations to herself. I will also encourage her and let her know how beautiful every part of her body is. She will live and not die to proclaim the Word of the Lord. And if by chance she goes on to be with You Lord, I will see her in glory because You have promised us everlasting life.

Matthews 9:35 *"And Jesus went about all the cities and villages, teaching in their synagogues, and preaching the gospel of the kingdom, and healing every sickness and every disease among the people."*

Genesis 42:2 *". . . that we may live, and not die."*

John 3:16 *"For God so loved the world, that he gave his only begotten Son, that whosoever believeth in him should not perish, but have everlasting life."*

II.   MY PRAYERS SHOULD NOT BE HINDERED

> *(I Peter 3:7b)* ". . . and as being heirs together of grace of like; that your prayers be not hindered."

> A.   Cause Her to Excel and Be Promoted Spiritually, Physically, and Mentally

> Jehovah Jira (Provider), as I lift my wife to You, I am looking for increase and an abundance to be in her and around her that it would be an overflow covering the entire family from generation to generation. Promotion comes from You, God, (from the North) so I am asking You to open doors for my wife that no man can shut and shut doors that no man can open. If there are any hindrances in her life, remove them. You said that you would remove every stumbling block that is in our way. Teach her your precepts that she will be a complete woman spiritually, physically, and mentally. Cause her life to be balanced at church, at home, at work, and even in her own business. Give her time and a desire to exercise so that she can keep her body toned. If she feels good about herself, she will not look down on others. She will be an encouragement to everyone around her. Bless her as she goes from level to level; from precept upon precept; line upon line; here a little, there a little; from strength to strength.

Isaiah 57:14 *"And shall say, Cast ye up, cast ye up, prepare the way, take up the stumblingblock out of the way of my people."*

Isaiah 28:10 *"For precept must be upon precept, precept upon precept; line upon line, line upon line; here a little, and there a little:"*

B.   Refresh, Revitalize, and Rejuvenate Her

El Shaddai (All Sufficient One), as the sun rises early in the morning from the East, replenish and refresh my wife that she may be rejuvenated. Whatever the locust, the palmerworm, and cankerworm came to eat up restore her. Replenish her in every area of her life. When she gets tired, give her a second wind to finish whatever project she needs to complete. As she goes through life's storms, bring her out whole. Move by Your Spirit, because it is not by power, nor by might, but it is by Your Spirit. Let her be like the tree that is planted by the rivers of water that brings forth its fruit in its season. As the storm comes and rage turbulence in her life, it will not break her down. When she goes through, bring her under the shadow of Your wings. Give her an anointing that will destroy every yoke of bondage. Rejuvenate her inner woman each and everyday of her life.

Joel 2:25 *"And I will restore to you the years that the locust hath eaten, the cankerworm, and the caterpiller, and the palmerworm, my great army which I sent among you."*

Psalms 1:3 *"And he shall be like a tree planted by the rivers of water, that bringeth forth his fruit in his season; his leaf also shall not wither; and whatsoever he doeth shall prosper."*

Isaiah 10:27 *"And it shall come to pass in that day, that his burden shall be taken away from off thy shoulder, and his yoke from off thy neck, and the yoke shall be destroyed because of the anointing."*

C. The Load That She Carries

Adonai (Lord, Master), all day everyday my wife has so much on her plate. She goes to work, takes care of the child(ren), cooks dinner, cleans the house, attends church services, PTA meetings, and then she has to meet my needs. She has so much to do in such little time that 24 hours is not enough time. Teach her how to cast her cares upon You for You careth for her. As she goes about her everyday responsibilities, give her the strength she needs to accomplish every task. Let me know what I need to do to assist her to make her load lighter. Give her the right words to say to me, that is very encouraging, that I can assist her and not want to run away to the rooftop. Sometimes when she is under pressure, she will say things that I know she doesn't mean. Show me exactly what she is trying to say and give me an ear that would be able to hear instructions from You to give her comfort especially when her load is heavy.

I Peter 5:7 *"Casting all your care upon him; for he careth for you."*

I Timothy 4:12 *"Let no man despise thy youth; but be thou an example of the believers, in word, in conversation, in charity, in spirit, in faith, in purity."*

I Peter 1:15 *"But as he which hath called you is holy, so be ye holy in all manner of conversation;"*

III. I WILL LOVE HER AS CHRIST LOVED THE
CHURCH

> *Ephesians 5:25* "Husbands, love
> your wives, even as Christ also
> loved the church, and gave
> himself for it;"

A.   God Created Her for Me

Jehovah Tsidkenu (The Lord Who is our Righteousness), You created my wife for me and sometimes it seems like the other way around. Plant in her heart a sweet desire toward me that she will love me when I am around and think about me when I am not. Before I come home show her how to set the ambience in the house for love. Give her the music she needs to play to set the atmosphere. Cause Your Holy Spirit to meet us there so that our lovemaking will be pure. I know this prayer might sound self-centered to some, however, God created my wife for me, and I want to love every part of her. I want her to tell me exactly what I need to do to fulfill her needs. Have her write me a love note and leave it on my pillar. When I arrive, I can read it and let it minister to my innerman. Cause Eros love to manifest to set the mood throughout our lovely home. Teach me not to only want her sexually, but want to love everything about her. I want to enjoy my wife so much that she will blossom like a flower in mid-summer.

Song of Solomon 4:9-10 *"Thou hast ravished my heart, my sister, my spouse; thou hast ravished my heart with one of thine eyes, with one chain of thy neck. How fair is thy love, my sister, my spouse! how much better is thy love than wine! and the smell of thine ointments than all spices!"*

Song of Solomon 2:8-11 *"The voice of my beloved! behold, he cometh leaping upon the mountains, skipping upon the hills.*

My beloved is like a rose or a young hart: behold, he standeth behind our wall, he looketh forth at the windows, shewing himself through the lattice. My beloved spake, and said unto me, Rise up, my love, my fair one, and come away. For, lo, the winter is past, the rain is over and gone;"

B.   I Will Prepare Her Meals

El Shaddai (God Almighty and a God that is more than enough), when she awakes in the morning on special occasions, let me have breakfast ready where I can feed her in bed, or show me that she has had enough and need me to pay more attention to her. Give me the words to say that they will comfort, edify and exalt her. I want to feed her spiritually, mentally and physically. I want to eat from Your spiritual table so that I can be healthy, dear Lord. Give her a prophetic word that would take her from a low state of mind to a higher state concerning her future. Give me the strength to take long walks and exercise with her. I want to satisfy my wife in every way. Show me areas where she is empty and lacking the nutrition that she needs, so that I can help meet the need. I want her to be healthy in every area of her life. Give me direction, so that her needs will always be met.

I Timothy 5:8 *"But if any provide not for his own, and specially for those of his own house, he hath denied the faith, and is worse than an infidel."*

Psalm 132:15 *"I will abundantly bless her provision: I will satisfy her poor with bread."*

C.   When She is Ill, I Will Take Care of Her

Jehovah Rapha (The Lord that Heals), You sent Your darling Son into the world to heal us from all sicknesses and diseases. For He (Jesus) was wounded for our transgression.

He was bruised for our iniquity. The chastisement of our peace was upon Him and by His stripes we are healed. If there is any form of sickness in my wife's body, I ask that You cut it out from the root. Send a divine healing from heaven that would heal her body. Show me what to do to help her feel better. Let me not disappear while she is not feeling well making excuses of things I have to do. Let me cater to her every need. Cause her body to function in the manner in which you intended. Healing is the children's bread. Also, it is Your desire that we prosper and be in health even as our soul prospers. Cause her to walk in Your light where she will stay close to the source. Let Your Word saturate her that she will know it as the power to heal.

Malachi 4:2 *"But unto you that fear my name shall the Sun of righteousness arise with healing in his wings; and ye shall go forth, and grow up as calves of the stall."*

Isaiah 53:4-5 *"Surely he hath borne our griefs, and carried our sorrows: yet we did esteem him stricken, smitten of God, and afflicted. But he was wounded for our transgressions, he was bruised for our iniquities: the chastisement of our peace was upon him; and with his stripes we are healed."*

III John 1:2 *"Beloved, I wish above all things that thou mayest prosper and be in health, even as thy soul prospereth."*

D. I Will Provide For Her

Jehovah Jira (Provider), I want to be in my rightful place for my family. I know divine order is what you expect from me. First it is You, Jesus, me, my wife and then my child(ren). If I am not working and in between jobs, I cannot provide for my wife the way You intended. I need You to open doors that no man can shut. I need to have an excellent salary with great benefits so that I can provide for my family. I want to have more than enough for the up building of your kingdom by paying my tithes and giving offerings. I want to owe no man so cause me to pay my bills off in full. Show me how to meet my wife's necessities and items she wants, buy the groceries and also save money for something to fall on. It seems like doors are being shut in my face, and I just cannot find a job or even the right job. I need a job that I enjoy doing or a business that I am passionate about. I don't want to work at a place where I am very unhappy which will cause me to be miserable. The result of being miserable is that I will bring it home and take it out on my family. Give me the skills, education, and trade I need to perform so that I can work in a pleasant environment. I want to be a provider for my family. Help me Lord. Open up the way for me and cause heaven to pour a release of increase to come my way. Let me not lack any good thing.

II Thessalonians 3:10 "*. . . if any would not work, neither should he eat.*"

Psalms 34:10 "*The young lions do lack, and suffer hunger: but they that seek the LORD shall not want any good thing.*"

IV. I WILL BE HER HUSBAND

Ephesians 5:33

> "Nevertheless let every one of you
> in particular so love his wife even
> as himself; and the wife see that
> she reverence her husband."

A. I Will Only Desire To Look To My Wife

Yahweh (Lord, Master - Omnipotence of God), when I look at my wife, I want to see her in a light where my heart melts. I ask that You forgive me for looking and/or thinking another woman can satisfy my needs. Let it be that my heart's desire will be toward my wife. Let me feel that she is the only woman that can fulfill my empty void from the seat of my affection. Quicken my spirit man when I am tempted to be with another. I don't want to burn in the bed of a harlot because once I sleep with a whoremonger, I am connected to her, but You can deliver me. You delivered me and set me free from my past, present and future sins. I thank you for it, Lord. By the blood of the Lamb, I destroy the spirit of adultery. I will teach my child(ren) the concept of one man to one woman. I know I married her for better or for worse. . . . When worse manifests, give me strength not to look toward another. In the book of James, he wrote we are tempted by the lust of our own eyes. I need You to keep me Lord that my relationship with my wife will be pure. I need You, Lord, in every area of my life to keep me on the right track. Let us trust one another and walk in your ordained precepts.

Titus 2:4-5 *"That they may teach the young women to be sober, to love their husbands, to love their children, To be discreet, chaste, keepers at home, good, obedient to their own husbands, that the word of God be not blasphemed."*

I Corinthians 7:3 *"Let the husband render unto the wife due benevolence: and likewise also the wife unto the husband."*

Proverbs 5:15 *"Drink waters out of thine own cistern, and running waters out of thine own well."*

B.   She Will Satisfy My Needs

El Elyon (The Most High God), When she kisses me, her love will taste better than my favorite juice drink. The scent of the bath beads she bathes in will be a good ointment like a virgin's love. I will lie between her breast and they will satisfy me. Everything that I need she will meet. Wherever I lack, she will pick up. She will complement me, and I will complement her. Also, the little things she does will satisfy me. When she prepares breakfast, lunch and dinner for me, it will supply me with the proper nutrition I need. If I need a button sewn on or some material mended, she will not let me look sloppy. In whatever area I need help in, she will come to help me. She won't take over, but assist me in getting things done. Make her an all around woman where she will be versatile and flexible. I am looking for her to grow and be able to teach our daughters how to be good wives and our sons what kind of wife they should look for in a woman. She will be the apple of my eye, and I will appreciate her. Even when she gets tired because of her busy schedule, she will lay next to me in our warm bed and that will satisfy us. When she is satisfied, it will satisfy me.

Proverbs 5:18-20 *"Let thy fountain be blessed: and rejoice with the wife of thy youth. Let her be as the loving hind and pleasant roe; let her breasts satisfy thee at all times; and be thou ravished always with her love. And why wilt thou, my son, be ravished with a strange woman, and embrace the bosom of a stranger?"*

Song of Solomon 1:13 *"A bundle of myrrh is my wellbeloved unto me; he shall lie all night betwixt my breasts."*

C.   My Heart Will Be Pure Toward Her

Oh Lord, create in me a pure heart and renew in me a right spirit. If there is any thing in my heart that is not right, remove it. Make my heart whiter than snow. For I know, as a man thinks in his heart so is he. I don't want any outside influences infiltrating my life to cause my relationship with my wife to be impure. I want to love her from sunup to sundown. I want our love to go from one level to another. Reveal to me her heart's desires where I may give of myself. Intensify our love each time we look at each other. Let her be the only woman for me, and show me how to keep her interest toward me. Cause us to trust one another. Let her not even question or insinuate that I might be dealing with another. Let me respect myself where I will show her respect. Show me how to have a good relationship with my mother, aunt and every female in my family. Cause unity to surround us for together we stand, divided we fall; woven us with the tapestry of love.

Colossians 3:18-19 *"Wives, submit yourselves unto your own husbands, as it is fit in the Lord. Husbands, love your wives, and be not bitter against them."*

Psalms 51:1-2 *"Have mercy upon me, O God, according to thy loving kindness: according unto the multitude of thy tender mercies blot out my transgressions. Wash me thoroughly from mine iniquity, and cleanse me from my sin."*

Psalms 51:7, 10 *"Purge me with hyssop, and I shall be clean: wash me, and I shall be whiter than snow. Create in me a clean heart, O God; and renew a right spirit within me."*

.... The effectual fervent prayer of a righteous man availeth much. (James 5:16) I thank you in advance for answering these prayers in Jesus' mighty name, Amen. AND IT IS SO!!!

V. CONCLUSION

My Heavenly Father, teach me Your precepts oh Lord, that I may know Your loving kindness. You are the Bridegroom who loves us. Show me exactly what I need to do to make her my true bride. Let me dress her in white linen, so that she will be draped with purity.

My lady is special and she deserves the best. Make me the man that can pregnant her with ideas that would cause us to flourish. Teach us to press toward the mark of the high calling which is in Christ Jesus; because the race is not given to the swift, or to the strong, but to the one that endures till the end.

Marriage is something to work on. I cannot expect to awake every morning and find a bed of ease, so teach me more prayers to pray for me, my wife, my child(ren) and even for other married couples all over the world.

Marriage ministries shall manifest all around to build the structure of the family again. Marriages are going to be reconciled. There is going to be a mighty healing in the area of relationships. God is looking to reconcile the family. He wants to mend the brokenness because He specializes in broken pieces.

PROPHETIC WORD FOR MEN

It is sometimes difficult for men to keep going and doing the things that are necessary for their families. The Lord wants to give them strength where they are weak and build them up where they might be torn down. He wants to shine His light on every dark place where the enemy will try to come in and set up camp.

To My Men of Honor:

I, God, designed you in such a way that you are already equipped to have dominion over your household and everything in the earth. I created you before I created woman because you and I have a special connection. I made you in my own image because I knew that just like me, you would visualize something and carry it in your heart and then you would speak great things into existence. But, over a period of time, you lost focus and started thinking in your own ability. You stopped looking to Me to make decisions for you. Some of you did not have a father figure to set an example for you, and some had a father living in the home. However, the father did not have a relationship with Me, so he couldn't teach you divine order. Some of you had father figures, but were so rebellious and disobedient, that you did what you wanted to do no matter what your father told you. <u>All that did not matter</u>. I still took care of your every need especially in your darkest hour. When I saw you thinking that you had failed in making right decisions, I, God, dispatched my messenger angels to bring you a rhema word in the night season to feed your spirit man, so that your natural man would be comforted. I opened doors for you, which you did not walk through because you started looking at your own ability and your own strength. Know this that I already made provision for you and went before you to make every crooked way straight. All I wanted is for you to take My yolk upon you and learn of Me, so that you would find rest unto your soul. You must begin to realize that it is My yolk that is easy and My burden that is light. I charge you now to go forth and be the man that I already ordained you to be before you were formed in your mother's womb. I will always come and meet you where you are, so that you will not have to struggle trying to reach for Me. I want you now from this day forward to cast all your cares upon me for I, God, cares for you. Everything you need is already in you. Tap into the treasures of life, so that you can see the life that I intended for you. Take my hand and let Me lead you from darkness into My marvelous light. (ref. Be Like A Tree, Planted ... pgs. 97-99)

Graciously speaking,

First Love, your Heavenly Father

Ephesians 5:24-33

"Therefore as the church is subject unto Christ, so let the wives be to their own husbands in everything. Husbands, love your wives, even as Christ also loved the church, and gave himself for it; That he might sanctify and cleanse it with the washing of water by the word, That he might present it to himself a glorious church, not having spot, or wrinkle, or any such thing; but that it should be holy and without blemish. So ought men to love their wives as their own bodies. He that loveth his wife loveth himself. For no man ever yet hated his own flesh; but nourisheth and cherisheth it, even as the Lord the church: For we are members of his body, of his flesh, and of his bones. For this cause shall a man leave his father and mother, and shall be joined unto his wife, and they two shall be one flesh. This is a great mystery: but I speak concerning Christ and the church. Nevertheless let every one of you in particular so love his wife even as himself; and the wife see that she reverence her husband."

LOVE HER AS YOU LOVE YOURSELF